THE

General Editor
R.B. Kennedy

Additional notes and editing
Mike Gould

MUCH ADO ABOUT NOTHING

William Shakespeare

COLLINS
CLASSICS

Harper Press
An imprint of HarperCollins*Publishers*
77–85 Fulham Palace Road
Hammersmith
London W6 8JB

This Harper Press paperback edition published 2011

A catalogue record for this book is available from the British Library

ISBN-13: 978-0-00-790241-5

Printed and bound in Great Britain by Clays Ltd, St Ives plc

MIX
Paper from responsible sources
FSC™ C007454

FSC™ is a non-profit international organisation established to promote the responsible management of the world's forests. Products carrying the FSC label are independently certified to assure consumers that they come from forests that are managed to meet the social, economic and ecological needs of present and future generations, and other controlled sources.

Find out more about HarperCollins and the environment at
www.harpercollins.co.uk/green

Life & Times section © Gerard Cheshire
Shakespeare: Words and Phrases adapted from
Collins English Dictionary
Typesetting in Kalix by Palimpsest Book Production Limited,
Falkirk, Stirlingshire

10 9 8 7 6 5 4 3 2 1

Prefatory Note

This Shakespeare play uses the full Alexander text. By keeping in mind the fact that the language has changed considerably in four hundred years, as have customs, jokes, and stage conventions, the editors have aimed at helping the modern reader – whether English is their mother tongue or not – to grasp the full significance of the play. The Notes, intended primarily for examination candidates, are presented in a simple, direct style. The needs of those unfamiliar with British culture have been specially considered.

Since quiet study of the printed word is unlikely to bring fully to life plays that were written directly for the public theatre, attention has been drawn to dramatic effects which are important in performance. The editors see Shakespeare's plays as living works of art which can be enjoyed today on stage, film and television in many parts of the world.

CONTENTS

An Elizabethan playhouse. Note the apron stage protruding into the auditorium, the space below it, the inner room at the rear of the stage, the gallery above the inner stage, the canopy over the main stage, and the absence of a roof over the audience.

The Theatre in Shakespeare's Day

On the face of it, the conditions in the Elizabethan theatre were not such as to encourage great writers. The public playhouse itself was not very different from an ordinary inn-yard; it was open to the weather; among the spectators were often louts, pickpockets and prostitutes; some of the actors played up to the rowdy elements in the audience by inserting their own jokes into the authors' lines, while others spoke their words loudly but unfeelingly; the presentation was often rough and noisy, with fireworks to represent storms and battles, and a table and a few chairs to represent a tavern; there were no actresses, so boys took the parts of women, even such subtle and mature ones as Cleopatra and Lady Macbeth; there was rarely any scenery at all in the modern sense. In fact, a quick inspection of the English theatre in the reign of Elizabeth I by a time-traveller from the twentieth century might well produce only one positive reaction: the costumes were often elaborate and beautiful.

Shakespeare himself makes frequent comments in his plays about the limitations of the playhouse and the actors of his time, often apologizing for them. At the beginning of *Henry V* the Prologue refers to the stage as 'this unworthy scaffold' and to the theatre building (the Globe, probably) as 'this wooden O', and emphasizes the urgent need for imagination in making up for all the deficiencies of presentation. In introducing Act IV the Chorus goes so far as to say:

> . . . we shall much disgrace
> With four or five most vile and ragged foils,
> Right ill-dispos'd in brawl ridiculous,
> The name of Agincourt, (lines 49–52)

In *A Midsummer Night's Dream* (Act V, Scene i) he seems to dismiss actors with the words:

The best in this kind are but shadows.

Yet Elizabeth's theatre, with all its faults, stimulated dramatists to a variety of achievement that has never been equalled and, in Shakespeare, produced one of the greatest writers in history. In spite of all his grumbles he seems to have been fascinated by the challenge that it presented him with. It is necessary to re-examine his theatre carefully in order to understand how he was able to achieve so much with the materials he chose to use. What sort of place was the Elizabethan playhouse in reality? What sort of people were these criticized actors? And what sort of audiences gave them their living?

The Development of the Theatre up to Shakespeare's Time

For centuries in England noblemen had employed groups of skilled people to entertain them when required. Under Tudor rule, as England became more secure and united, actors such as these were given more freedom, and they often performed in public, while still acknowledging their 'overlords' (in the 1570s, for example, when Shakespeare was still a schoolboy at Stratford, one famous company was called 'Lord Leicester's Men'). London was rapidly becoming larger and more important in the second half of the sixteenth century, and many of the companies of actors took the opportunities offered to establish themselves at inns on the main roads leading to the City (for example, the Boar's Head in Whitechapel and the Tabard in South-wark) or in the City itself. These groups of actors would come to an agreement with the inn-keeper which would give them the use of the yard for their performances after people had eaten and drunk well in the middle of the day. Before long, some inns were taken over completely by companies of players and thus became the first public theatres. In 1574 the officials of the City of London issued an order which shows clearly that these theatres were both popular and also offensive to some respectable people, because the order complains about 'the inordinate haunting of great multitudes of people, specially youth, to plays interludes and shows; namely occasion of frays and quarrels, evil practices of incontinency in great inns . . .' There is evidence that, on public holidays, the theatres on the banks of the Thames were crowded with noisy apprentices and tradesmen, but it would be wrong to think that audiences were always undiscriminating and loudmouthed. In spite of the disapproval of Puritans and the more staid members of society, by the 1590s, when Shakespeare's plays were beginning to be performed, audiences consisted of a good cross-section of English society, nobility as well as workers, intellectuals as well as simple people out for a laugh; also (and in this respect English theatres were unique in Europe), it was quite normal for respectable women to attend plays. So Shakespeare had to write plays which would appeal to people of widely different kinds. He had to provide 'something for everyone' but at the same time to take care to unify the material so that it would not seem to fall into separate pieces as they watched it. A speech like that of the drunken porter in *Macbeth* could provide the 'groundlings' with a belly-laugh, but also held a deeper significance for those who could appreciate it. The audience he wrote for was one of a number of apparent drawbacks which Shakespeare was able to turn to his and our advantage.

Shakespeare's Actors

Nor were all the actors of the time mere 'rogues, vagabonds and sturdy beggars' as some were described in a Statute of 1572. It is true that many of them had a hard life and earned very little money, but leading actors could become partners in the ownership of the theatres in which they acted: Shakespeare was a shareholder in the Globe and the Blackfriars theatres when he was an actor as well as a playwright. In any case, the attacks made on Elizabethan actors were usually directed at their morals and not at their acting ability; it is clear that many of them must have been good at their trade if they were able to interpret complex works like the great tragedies in such a way as to attract enthusiastic audiences. Undoubtedly some of the boys took the women's parts with skill and confidence, since a man called Coryate, visiting Venice in 1611, expressed surprise that women could act as well as they: 'I saw women act, a thing that I never saw before . . . and they performed it with as good a grace, action, gesture . . . as ever I saw any masculine actor.' The quality of most of the actors who first presented Shakespeare's plays is probably accurately summed up by Fynes Moryson, who wrote, '. . . as there be, in my opinion, more plays in London than in all the parts of the world I have seen, so do these players or comedians excel all other in the world.'

The Structure of the Public Theatre

Although the 'purpose-built' theatres were based on the inn-yards which had been used for play-acting, most of them were circular. The walls contained galleries on three storeys from which the wealthier patrons watched, they must have been something like the 'boxes' in a modern theatre, except that they held much larger numbers – as many as 1500. The 'groundlings' stood on the floor of the building, facing a raised stage which projected from the 'stage-wall', the main features of which were:

1. a small room opening on to the back of the main stage and on the same level as it (rear stage),
2. a gallery above this inner stage (upper stage),
3. canopy projecting from above the gallery over the main stage, to protect the actors from the weather (the 700 or 800 members of the audience who occupied the yard, or 'pit' as we call it today, had the sky above them).

In addition to these features there were dressing-rooms behind the stage and a space underneath it from which entrances could be made through trap-doors. All the acting areas – main stage, rear stage, upper stage and under stage – could be entered by actors directly from their dressing rooms, and all of them were used in productions of Shakespeare's plays. For example, the inner stage, an almost cavelike structure, would have been where Ferdinand and Miranda are 'discovered' playing chess in the last act of *The Tempest*, while the upper stage was certainly the balcony from which Romeo climbs down in Act III of *Romeo and Juliet.*

It can be seen that such a building, simple but adaptable, was not really unsuited to the presentation of plays like Shakespeare's. On the contrary, its simplicity guaranteed the minimum of distraction, while its shape and construction must have produced a sense of involvement on the part of the audience that modern producers would envy.

Other Resources of the Elizabethan Theatre

Although there were few attempts at scenery in the public theatre (painted backcloths were occasionally used in court performances), Shakespeare and his fellow playwrights were able to make use of a fair variety of 'properties', lists of such articles have survived: they include beds, tables, thrones, and also trees, walls, a gallows, a Trojan horse and a 'Mouth of Hell'; in a list of properties belonging to the manager, Philip Henslowe, the curious item 'two mossy banks' appears. Possibly one of them was used for the

> bank whereon the wild thyme blows,
> Where oxlips and the nodding violet grows

in *A Midsummer Night's Dream* (Act II, Scene i). Once again, imagination must have been required of the audience.

Costumes were the one aspect of stage production in which

trouble and expense were hardly ever spared to obtain a magnificent effect. Only occasionally did they attempt any historical accuracy (almost all Elizabethan productions were what we should call 'modern-dress' ones), but they were appropriate to the characters who wore them: kings were seen to be kings and beggars were similarly unmistakable. It is an odd fact that there was usually no attempt at illusion in the costuming: if a costume looked fine and rich it probably was. Indeed, some of the costumes were almost unbelievably expensive. Henslowe lent his company £19 to buy a cloak, and the Alleyn brothers, well-known actors, gave £20 for a 'black velvet cloak, with sleeves embroidered all with silver and gold, lined with black satin striped with gold'.

With the one exception of the costumes, the 'machinery' of the playhouse was economical and uncomplicated rather than crude and rough, as we can see from this second and more leisurely look at it. This meant that playwrights were stimulated to produce the imaginative effects that they wanted from the language that they used. In the case of a really great writer like Shakespeare, when he had learned his trade in the theatre as an actor, it seems that he received quite enough assistance of a mechanical and structural kind without having irksome restrictions and conventions imposed on him; it is interesting to try to guess what he would have done with the highly complex apparatus of a modern television studio. We can see when we look back to his time that he used his instrument, the Elizabethan theatre, to the full, but placed his ultimate reliance on the communication between his imagination and that of his audience through the medium of words. It is, above all, his rich and wonderful use of language that must have made play-going at that time a memorable experience for people of widely different kinds. Fortunately, the deep satisfaction of appreciating and enjoying Shakespeare's work can be ours also, if we are willing to overcome the language difficulty produced by the passing of time.

Shakespeare: A Timeline

Very little indeed is known about Shakespeare's private life; the facts included here are almost the only indisputable ones. The dates of Shakespeare's plays are those on which they were first produced.

1558	Queen Elizabeth crowned.	
1561	Francis Bacon born.	
1564	Christopher Marlowe born.	William Shakespeare born, April 23rd, baptized April 26th.
1566		Shakespeare's brother, Gilbert, born.
1567	Mary, Queen of Scots, deposed. James VI (later James I of England) crowned King of Scotland.	
1572	Ben Jonson born. Lord Leicester's Company (of players) licensed; later called Lord Strange's, then the Lord Chamberlain's and finally (under James) the King's Men.	
1573	John Donne born.	
1574	The Common Council of London directs that all plays and playhouses in London must be licensed.	
1576	James Burbage builds the first public playhouse, The Theatre, at Shoreditch, outside the walls of the City.	
1577	Francis Drake begins his voyage round the world (completed 1580). *Holinshed's Chronicles of England, Scotland and Ireland* published (which	

	Shakespeare later used extensively).	
1582		Shakespeare married to Anne Hathaway.
1583	The Queen's Company founded by royal warrant.	Shakespeare's daughter, Susanna, born.
1585		Shakespeare's twins, Hamnet and Judith, born.
1586	Sir Philip Sidney, the Elizabethan ideal 'Christian knight', poet, patron, soldier, killed at Zutphen in the Low Countries.	
1587	Mary, Queen of Scots, beheaded. Marlowe's *Tamburlaine (Part I)* first staged.	
1588	Defeat of the Spanish Armada. Marlowe's *Tamburlaine (Part II)* first staged.	
1589	Marlowe's *Jew of Malta* and Kyd's *Spanish Tragedy* (a 'revenge tragedy' and one of the most popular plays of Elizabethan times).	
1590	Spenser's *Faerie Queene* (Books I–III) published.	
1592	Marlowe's *Doctor Faustus* and *Edward II* first staged. Witchcraft trials in Scotland. Robert Greene, a rival playwright, refers to Shakespeare as 'an upstart crow' and 'the only Shake-scene in a country'.	*Titus Andronicus* *Henry VI, Parts I, II and III* *Richard III*
1593	London theatres closed by the plague. Christopher Marlowe killed in a Deptford tavern.	*Two Gentlemen of Verona* *Comedy of Errors* *The Taming of the Shrew* *Love's Labour's Lost*
1594	Shakespeare's company becomes The Lord Chamberlain's Men.	*Romeo and Juliet*

1595	Raleigh's first expedition to Guiana. Last expedition of Drake and Hawkins (both died).	*Richard II* *A Midsummer Night's Dream*
1596	Spenser's *Faerie Queene* (Books IV–VI) published. James Burbage buys rooms at Blackfriars and begins to convert them into a theatre.	*King John* *The Merchant of Venice* Shakespeare's son Hamnet dies. Shakespeare's father is granted a coat of arms.
1597	James Burbage dies, his son Richard, a famous actor, turns the Blackfriars Theatre into a private playhouse.	*Henry IV (Part I)* Shakespeare buys and redecorates New Place at Stratford.
1598	Death of Philip II of Spain	*Henry IV (Part II)* *Much Ado About Nothing*
1599	Death of Edmund Spenser. The Globe Theatre completed at Bankside by Richard and Cuthbert Burbage.	*Henry V* *Julius Caesar* *As You Like It*
1600	Fortune Theatre built at Cripplegate. East India Company founded for the extension of English trade and influence in the East. The Children of the Chapel begin to use the hall at Blackfriars.	*Merry Wives of Windsor* *Troilus and Cressida*
1601		*Hamlet*
1602	Sir Thomas Bodley's library opened at Oxford.	*Twelfth Night*
1603	Death of Queen Elizabeth. James I comes to the throne. Shakespeare's company becomes The King's Men. Raleigh tried, condemned and sent to the Tower	
1604	Treaty of peace with Spain	*Measure for Measure* *Othello* *All's Well that Ends Well*
1605	The Gunpowder Plot: an attempt by a group of Catholics to blow up the Houses of Parliament.	

1606	Guy Fawkes and other plotters executed.	*Macbeth* *King Lear*
1607	Virginia, in America, colonized. A great frost in England.	*Antony and Cleopatra* *Timon of Athens* *Coriolanus* Shakespeare's daughter, Susanna, married to Dr. John Hall.
1608	The company of the Children of the Chapel Royal (who had performed at Blackfriars for ten years) is disbanded. John Milton born. Notorious pirates executed in London.	Richard Burbage leases the Blackfriars Theatre to six of his fellow actors, including Shakespeare. *Pericles, Prince of Tyre*
1609		Shakespeare's Sonnets published.
1610	A great drought in England	*Cymbeline*
1611	Chapman completes his great translation of the *Iliad*, the story of Troy. Authorized Version of the Bible published.	*A Winter's Tale* *The Tempest*
1612	Webster's *The White Devil* first staged.	Shakespeare's brother, Gilbert, dies.
1613	Globe theatre burnt down during a performance of *Henry VIII* (the firing of small cannon set fire to the thatched roof). Webster's *Duchess of Malfi* first staged.	*Henry VIII* *Two Noble Kinsmen* Shakespeare buys a house at Blackfriars.
1614	Globe Theatre rebuilt in 'far finer manner than before'.	
1616	Ben Jonson publishes his plays in one volume. Raleigh released from the Tower in order to prepare an expedition to the gold mines of Guiana.	Shakespeare's daughter, Judith, marries Thomas Quiney. Death of Shakespeare on his birthday, April 23rd.
1618	Raleigh returns to England and is executed on the charge for which he was imprisoned in 1603.	
1623	Publication of the Folio edition of Shakespeare's plays	Death of Anne Shakespeare (née Hathaway).

Life & Times

William Shakespeare the Playwright

There exists a curious paradox when it comes to the life of William Shakespeare. He easily has more words written about him than any other famous English writer, yet we know the least about him. This inevitably means that most of what is written about him is either fabrication or speculation. The reason why so little is known about Shakespeare is that he wasn't a novelist or a historian or a man of letters. He was a playwright, and playwrights were considered fairly low on the social pecking order in Elizabethan society. Writing plays was about providing entertainment for the masses – the great unwashed. It was the equivalent to being a journalist for a tabloid newspaper.

In fact, we only know of Shakespeare's work because two of his friends had the foresight to collect his plays together following his death and have them printed. The only reason they did so was apparently because they rated his talent and thought it would be a shame if his words were lost.

Consequently his body of work has ever since been assessed and reassessed as the greatest contribution to English literature. That is despite the fact that we know that different printers took it upon themselves to heavily edit the material they worked from. We also know that Elizabethan plays were worked and reworked frequently, so that they evolved over time until they were honed to perfection, which means that many different hands played their part in the active writing process. It would therefore be fair to say that any play attributed to Shakespeare is unlikely to contain a great deal of original input. Even the plots were based on well known historical events, so it would be hard to know what fragments of any Shakespeare play came from that single mind.

One might draw a comparison with the Christian bible, which remains such a compelling read because it came from the collaboration of many contributors and translators over centuries, who each adjusted the stories until they could no longer be improved. As virtually nothing is known of Shakespeare's life and even less about his method of working, we shall never know the truth about his plays. They certainly contain some very elegant phrasing, clever plot devices and plenty of words never before seen in print, but as to whether Shakespeare invented them from a unique imagination or whether he simply took them from others around him is anyone's guess.

The best bet seems to be that Shakespeare probably took the lead role in devising the original drafts of the plays, but was open to collaboration from any source when it came to developing them into workable scripts for effective performances. He would have had to work closely with his fellow actors in rehearsals, thereby finding out where to edit, abridge, alter, reword and so on.

In turn, similar adjustments would have occurred in his absence, so that definitive versions of his plays never really existed. In effect Shakespeare was only responsible for providing the framework of plays, upon which others took liberties over time. This wasn't helped by the fact that the English language itself was not definitive at that time either. The consequence was that people took it upon themselves to spell words however they pleased or to completely change words and phrasing to suit their own preferences.

It is easy to see then, that Shakespeare's plays were always going to have lives of their own, mutating and distorting in detail like Chinese whispers. The culture of creative preservation was simply not established in Elizabethan England. Creative ownership of Shakespeare's plays was lost to him as soon as he released them into the consciousness of others. They saw nothing wrong with taking his ideas and running with them, because no one had ever suggested that one shouldn't, and Shakespeare probably regarded his work in the same way. His plays weren't sacrosanct works of art, they were templates for theatre folk to make their livings from, so they had every right to mould them into productions that drew in the crowds as effectively as possible. Shakespeare was like the helmsman of a sailing ship, steering the vessel but wholly reliant on the team work of his crew to arrive at the desired destination.

It seems that Shakespeare certainly had a natural gift, but the genius of his plays may be attributable to the collective efforts of Shakespeare and others. It is a rather satisfying notion to think that *his* plays might actually be the creative outpourings of the Elizabethan milieu in which Shakespeare immersed himself. That makes them important social documents as well as seminal works of the English language.

Money in Shakespeare's Day

It is extremely difficult, if not impossible, to relate the value of money in our time to its value in another age and to compare prices of commodities today and in the past. Many items *are* simply not comparable on grounds of quality or serviceability.

There was a bewildering variety of coins in use in Elizabethan England. As nearly all English and European coins were gold or silver, they had intrinsic value apart from their official value. This meant that foreign coins circulated freely in England and were officially recognized, for example the French crown (écu) worth about 30p (72 cents), and the Spanish ducat worth about 33p (79 cents). The following table shows some of the coins mentioned by Shakespeare and their relation to one another.

GOLD	*British*	*American*	SILVER	*British*	*American*
sovereign (heavy type)	£1.50	$3.60	shilling	10p	24c
sovereign (light type)	66p–£l	$1.58–$2.40	groat	1.5p	4c
angel					
royal	33p–50p	79c–$1.20			
noble	50p	$1.20			
crown	25p	60c			

A comparison of the following prices in Shakespeare's time with the prices of the same items today will give some idea of the change in the value of money.

ITEM	PRICE *British*	*American*	ITEM	PRICE *British*	*American*
beef, per lb.	0.5p	1c	cherries (lb.)	1p	2c
mutton, leg	7.5p	18c	7 oranges	1p	2c
rabbit	3.5p	9c	1 lemon	1p	2c
chicken	3p	8c	cream (quart)	2.5p	6c
potatoes (lb)	10p	24c	sugar (lb.)	£1	$2.40
carrots (bunch)	1p	2c	sack (wine) (gallon)	14p	34c
8 artichokes	4p	9c	tobacco (oz.)	25p	60c
1 cucumber	1p	2c	biscuits (lb.)	12.5p	30c

INTRODUCTION

We don't know exactly when *Much Ado About Nothing* was written or first performed but it does seem likely that Shakespeare composed it before 1600, with the first known performance being in 1613. The play was very popular then and remains so today, possibly due to themes and characters which are recognisable to us all – the two apparent enemies who desperately feed off each other's company and fall in love; the jealous young man and the innocent bride-to-be, victim of a bitter rival's cunning; the shamed father who has seen his well-made plans for the future come to nothing (or so it seems), and bumbling twits who unwittingly hold the key to clearing up the mess. Add to this cocktail various disguises, tricks, mistakes, sexy (even rude) jokes and several highly-dramatic moments – and it's not difficult to see why the play remains a hit with audiences.

We tend to think of the play as a comedy – it ends with two marriages, and the 'loose ends' are largely tied-up, but is this all it is about? At the heart of the play is quite an unpleasant scene as Claudio rejects Hero, calling her a 'rotten orange', believing her to be permanently damaged goods – a 'common stale'. Can this be the same man who called her a 'jewel' only a little earlier? Claudio, despite all the reports of him as a noble young man who has performed bravely in Don Pedro's service, can come out of the play as the worst sort of young, inexperienced fool – all too ready to think the worst of women. Add to this Hero's father's shame and his concern, perhaps, for his own reputation first and foremost, and we get an insight into Shakespeare's times when marriage was a contract and a negotiation, and children – especially young women – were properties to be exchanged and sold.

Yet to focus on this darker side would, in the end, to

be to deny the laughter, wit and sheer liveliness of the story. The two characters who are at its centre – Beatrice and Benedick – delight us with their quick exchanges, and we are ultimately moved when the two people who have expressed the least faith in love and commitment, find themselves hopelessly devoted to each other.

The play itself seems to be based on an Italian tale called *Timbreo di Cardona* by Bandello. In one version of the tale, Claudio is recognisable in the character of Timbreo and Hero is named Fenicia. One clue to where Shakespeare sourced his idea for Don John's bitterness and spite, comes in this story. Girondo (the Don John character) is Timbreo's companion and falls in love with Fenicia, but she rejects him, and this is what leads to him trying to ruin her relationship with Timbreo. This does not happen in *Much Ado about Nothing* – it seems Don John's envy has other roots, but some productions do choose to suggest he is keen on Hero, to give his spite more meaning and motive.

The Plot

ACT 1

Scene 1

The play begins in front of the house of Leonato, Governor of Messina. A messenger brings word to him that Don Pedro of Aragon is to arrive at Messina returning from a victorious battle. Beatrice, Leonato's niece, asks if Benedick, a bachelor whom she has met before, is part of the company and hides her interest with cutting remarks about him. Don Pedro, Don John (his illegitimate brother) Claudio, and Benedick arrive. Beatrice and Benedick trade insults, while Claudio, attracted by Hero's beauty, thinks he has fallen in love. He asks Benedick what he thinks of the lady, but Benedick says that marriage is for fools and criticises womankind.

Don Pedro, however, supports Claudio, and says he will disguise himself and speak to Hero and her father during the masked ball that evening.

Scene 2

Antonio reports to his brother Leonato that he has overheard Don Pedro telling Claudio that he is in love with Hero. Leonato says that he'll wait to hear this from Don Pedro, but will tell his daughter about the Prince's intentions.

Scene 3

Don John speaks with Conrade, one of his followers, explaining why he acts in the way he does ('I cannot hide what I am: I must be sad when I have cause.'). Conrade advises him to act in a civil way to his brother. After all, he has been forgiven his rebellion against him. Borachio, another of Don John's men, arrives. He tells Don John that he has overheard news of the intended marriage of Claudio and Hero. Don John says that there might be opportunities in this to make mischief for Claudio, whom he dislikes as he thinks has taken his place in his brother's affections.

ACT 2

Scene 1

Leonato, Hero and Beatrice prepare for the party to begin. Beatrice complains that there is no man who can match her spirit, but Hero obediently agrees to her father's request to accept the Prince. They put on masks for the dance which leads to confusion and fun. Don Pedro talks to Hero privately while Benedick and Beatrice, behind their masks, insult each other. Meanwhile, Don John makes Claudio jealous by saying that Don Pedro plans to wed Hero himself. Claudio thinks he has lost Hero. However, Don Pedro tells Claudio that all is well, and that Hero has agreed to marry him. Claudio's jealousy turns to joy. Now that the wedding is arranged, Don Pedro decides to find a husband for Beatrice. He believes that Benedick would be ideal. All present agree that they will trick Beatrice and Benedick into falling in love with one another.

Scene 2

However, Borachio now suggests a darker plot to ruin Claudio's marriage plans. Borachio will arrange to meet with Margaret, Hero's gentlewoman, at Hero's window in the middle of the night. This will fool the Duke and Claudio into believing that Hero is having an affair. Don John is so keen on the idea of creating mischief for Claudio that he promises Borachio 1000 ducats.

Scene 3

Benedick is in the garden considering Claudio's sudden change from soldier to dopey lover when Don Pedro, Claudio, and Leonato approach. He hides behind some trees, but he doesn't realise they have seen him. Then, for Benedick's benefit, they announce that Beatrice loves him. But they also say they are worried that Benedick will just make fun of her if he finds out. Benedick is utterly fooled. By the end of the scene, he is weighing up the benefits of marriage and reflecting on his past behaviour. So, when Beatrice arrives to call him in to dinner, his new-found love for her makes him believe her sharp comments are actually declarations of love.

ACT 3

Scene 1

Hero arranges for Beatrice to overhear a conversation about Benedick's love sickness and desire for Beatrice. Beatrice listens while Hero and her waiting lady, Ursula, discuss how Beatrice would only make fun of Benedick if she knew. Beatrice is fooled and vows to love Benedick if he will have her.

Scene 2

Don Pedro, Claudio, and Leonato make fun of Benedick saying he looks pale and depressed – as well as clean and newly-shaven, and tell him he must be in love. Benedick has soon had enough of their teasing, and leaves to speak privately with Leonato. Don John joins Don Pedro and Claudio and accuses Hero of being unfaithful. He says he wants to save Claudio from a shameful marriage, and he will prove her disloyalty. Don John says he will take them that night to Hero's bedroom window where they will see her with another lover, the very night before her wedding. Claudio swears that if it turns out to be true, he will shame her at their wedding in front of the whole congregation.

Scene 3

The Watch (local police) assembles and gets muddled instructions from Dogberry and Verges to be alert for enemies of the prince. They overhear Borachio boast to Conrade about how he has just earned a thousand ducats from Don John. He explains that he did this by fooling Claudio and Don Pedro into believing that Hero met with him at her window. He had in fact met with Hero's maid Margaret. The watch officers step forward and arrest Borachio and Conrade for their crime.

Scene 4

Hero prepares nervously for her wedding, saying her 'heart is exceedingly heavy' (does she sense that not everything will go to plan?). Beatrice arrives, but seems distracted – saying she herself is 'exceeding ill' and 'sick'. Margaret teases Beatrice, saying she might be in love, just like Benedick.

Scene 5

The Constable Dogberry meets with Leonato to tell him the Watch has taken two prisoners during the night, and they need to be questioned. Unfortunately, Leonato is in a hurry to leave for the church with Hero and can't make sense out of Dogberry's and Verges' confusing explanation (they claim to have 'comprehended' two villains, when of course they mean 'apprehended') Leonato orders them to carry out the interrogation themselves.

ACT 4

Scene 1

Everyone meets at the church for the wedding of Hero and Claudio. When the friar asks Claudio if he is there to marry Hero, he says no. He then tells Leonato to take his daughter back, because she has betrayed him with another man. Claudio says he has proof she is unfaithful, and Don Pedro and Don John back up his accusations. Hero faints, and Don John, Pedro and Claudio leave. For a moment there is a thought she may be dead, but she recovers. Beatrice, Benedick, Leonato, and the friar begin to suspect that Don John is behind the accusations. The Friar suggests they let people think Hero has died. Claudio will begin to feel guilty and in the meantime they will try to find out the truth. Left alone together Benedick confesses his love to Beatrice, who finally admits that she loves him also. To prove his love, Beatrice asks Benedick to take revenge for the wrong done to Hero. He agrees to challenge Claudio.

Scene 2

The Constables meet and form a 'dissembly' (they mean 'assembly' of course) to interrogate Borachio and Conrade. Despite the confusion caused by Dogberry's misuse of words and phrases, the Sexton successfully accuses Borachio and Conrade of plotting against Hero, who everyone believes to be dead. We are also told that Don John has secretly fled.

ACT 5

Scene 1

Leonato angrily confronts Don Pedro and Claudio and then challenges Claudio to a duel to regain the honour of his daughter. Antonio, Leonato's brother, joins in the challenge, but Claudio and Pedro refuse to fight. Antonio and Leonato leave, vowing revenge. Benedick then appears, and also challenges Claudio to a duel for the honour of Hero. Claudio and Don Pedro make fun of him, thinking he is joking, but as he leaves he tells Don Pedro that his brother, Don John, has fled Messina and that they have falsely accused and killed an innocent lady.

The constables appear and Don Pedro and Claudio are shocked when they find out from them about Don John's villainy. Claudio remembers how he first loved Hero. Leonato hears the news about Don John, but rather than blaming him or Borachio, he says Pedro and Claudio are the real villains. They are the ones who caused the death of Hero by believing what was said about her. They beg Leonato to punish them in whatever way he chooses. Leonato commands them to proclaim Hero's innocence to the people of Messina. Also, Claudio must marry another niece of his the following day, as a sort of sign of his respect for Leonato's family.

Scene 2

Benedick meets with Beatrice and they repeat their love for each other. Benedick tells Beatrice he has challenged Claudio, but then Ursula, the lady's gentlewoman, enters and tells them that Don John was behind everything – though he has now fled.

Scene 3

Claudio and Don Pedro come with lighted candles to Leonato's family monument. Claudio recites an epitaph (a verse on someone's death) to Hero and they remain there, keeping until morning.

Scene 4
While Leonato awaits Claudio's arrival Benedick asks the friar if he will marry him and Beatrice. The women come forward masked. Claudio (believing he is marrying Leonato's other niece) declares himself husband to the woman he stands beside, and Hero reveals herself. Beatrice and Benedick argue about whether they really love one another, but their friends produce secret poems each has written declaring how they feel which proves their true emotions. Benedick kisses Beatrice to stop her jokes and teasing, and all are joined together in a dance to celebrate the two marriages. The play ends with the news that Don John has been captured, and has been brought back to Messina, but Benedick says they should not think about him till the next day. In the meantime, there should be music and dance.

LIST OF CHARACTERS

Don Pedro	Prince of Arragon
Don John	his bastard brother
Claudio	a young lord of Florence
Benedick	a young lord of Padua
Leonato	Governor of Messina
Antonio	his brother
Balthasar	attendant on Don Pedro
Borachio *Conrade*	followers of Don John
Friar Francis	
Dogberry	a constable
Verges	a headborough
A Sexton	
A Boy	
Hero	daughter to Leonato
Beatrice	niece to Leonato
Margaret *Ursula*	gentlewomen attending on Hero

Messengers, a *Watch*, and *Attendants*

The Scene: Messina

ACT I SCENE I

The opening scene, one of excited news and anticipation, explains the situation (the arrival of Don Pedro and his company, the previous relationship between Benedick and Beatrice) and establishes the key characters (only characters such as Dogberry are missing) and their relationships. We even learn something about Don John, through his lack of language – is he already set apart from everyone else? In addition, the action is kick-started as Claudio falls for Hero and Don Pedro offers to woo on his young companion's behalf.

3. ***by this*** by now.
3. ***league*** three miles.
5. ***action*** minor battle.

6. ***sort*** high rank.
6. ***of name*** well-known.

11. ***remembered*** rewarded.
12. ***borne*** himself behaved.
13. ***figure*** appearance.
14. ***feats*** achievements.

21. ***badge*** sign.

ACT ONE

Scene I

Before Leonato's house.

[Enter LEONATO, HERO, *and* BEATRICE, *with a* MESSENGER.*]*

Leonato

I learn in this letter that Don Pedro of Arragon comes this night to Messina.

Messenger

He is very near by this; he was not three leagues off when I left him.

Leonato

How many gentlemen have you lost in this action?

Messenger

But few of any sort, and none of name.

Leonato

A victory is twice itself when the achiever brings home full numbers. I find here that Don Pedro hath bestowed much honour on a young Florentine called Claudio.

Messenger

Much deserv'd on his part, and equally remembʼred by Don Pedro. He hath borne himself beyond the promise of his age, doing, in the figure of a lamb, the feats of a lion; he hath, indeed, better bettʼred expectation than you must expect of me to tell you how.

Leonato

He hath an uncle here in Messina will be very much glad of it.

Messenger

I have already delivered him letters, and there appears much joy in him; even so much that joy could not show itself modest enough without a badge of bitterness.

25. ***kind*** natural, instinctive.

28. ***Mountanto*** duellist, fencer.

35. ***set up his bills*** posted notices.
36. ***at the flight*** to an archery contest.
37. ***subscribed for*** took the part of.
38. ***bird-bolt*** short blunt arrow.
38. ***pray*** ask.

42. ***tax*** accuse.
43. ***be meet*** get even.

45. ***musty*** victual stale food.
45. ***holp*** helped.
46. ***trencherman*** person with a hearty appetite.

Leonato
Did he break out into tears?

Messenger
In great measure.

Leonato
A kind overflow of kindness. There are no faces truer than those that are so wash'd. How much better is it to weep at joy than to joy at weeping!

Beatrice
I pray you, is Signior Mountanto returned from the wars or no?

Messenger
I know none of that name, lady; there was none such in the army of any sort.

Leonato
What is he that you ask for, niece?

Hero
My cousin means Signior Benedick of Padua.

Messenger
O, he's return'd, and as pleasant as ever he was.

Beatrice
He set up his bills here in Messina, and challeng'd Cupid at the flight; and my uncle's fool, reading the challenge, subscrib'd for Cupid, and challenge him at the bird-bolt. I pray you, how many hath he kill'd and eaten in these wars? But how many hath he kill'd? For, indeed, I promised to eat all of his killing.

Leonato
Faith, niece, you tax Signior Benedick too much; but he'll be meet with you, I doubt it not.

Messenger
He hath done good service, lady, in these wars.

Beatrice
You had musty victual, and he hath holp to eat it; he is a very valiant trencherman; he hath an excellent stomach.

51. ***stuffed man*** tailor's model/dummy (i.e. one that is stuffed so that it resembles a real person).

55. ***mistake*** misunderstand.
56. ***betwixt*** between.
57. ***skirmish*** battle.

59. ***Alas*** unfortunately.
60. ***wits*** parts of the mind.
60. ***halting*** limping.

70. ***block*** wooden mould used to style a hat (suggests his faith swings whichever way fashion goes).
71. ***in your books*** in favour with you.
72. ***an*** if.

73. ***study*** library.
74. ***squarer*** hooligan.

Messenger

And a good soldier too, lady.

Beatrice

And a good soldier to a lady; but what is he to a lord?

Messenger

A lord to a lord, a man to a man; stuff'd with all honourable virtues.

Beatrice

It is so, indeed; he is no less than a stuff'd man; but for the stuffing – well, we are all mortal.

Leonato

You must not, sir, mistake my niece: there is a kind of merry war betwixt Signior Benedick and her; they never meet but there's a skirmish of wit between them.

Beatrice

Alas, he gets nothing by that. In our last conflict four of his five wits went halting off, and now is the whole man govern'd with one; so that if he have wit enough to keep himself warm, let him bear it for a difference between himself and his horse; for it is all the wealth that he hath left, to be known a reasonable creature. Who is his companion now? He hath every month a new sworn brother.

Messenger

Is't possible?

Beatrice

Very easily possible: he wears his faith but as the fashion of his hat; it ever changes with the next block.

Messenger

I see, lady, the gentleman is not in your books.

Beatrice

No; an he were, I would burn my study. But, I pray you, who is his companion? Is there no young squarer now that will make a voyage with him to the devil?

79. ***pestilence*** plague.
79. ***taker*** victim of the disease.
80. ***presently*** immediately.
82. ***ere 'a be*** before he is.

87. ***is approached*** has arrived.

91. ***likeness*** appearance.

94. ***abides*** remains.

95. ***charge*** expense, trouble.

Messenger

He is most in the company of the right noble Claudio.

Beatrice

O Lord! He will hang upon him like a disease; he is sooner caught than the pestilence, and the taker runs presently mad. God help the noble Claudio! If he have caught the Benedick, it will cost him a thousand pound ere 'a be cured.

Messenger

I will hold friends with you, lady.

Beatrice

Do, good friend.

Leonato

You will never run mad, niece.

Beatrice

No, not till a hot January.

Messenger

Don Pedro is approach'd.

[Enter DON PEDRO, CLAUDIO, BENEDICK, BALTHASAR, *and* JOHN THE BASTARD.*]*

Don Pedro

Good Signior Leonato, are you come to meet your trouble? The fashion of the world is to avoid cost, and you encounter it.

Leonato

Never came trouble to my house in the likeness of your Grace; for trouble being gone comfort should remain; but when you depart from me sorrow abides, and happiness takes his leave.

Don Pedro

You embrace your charge too willingly. I think this is your daughter.

Leonato

Her mother hath many times told me so.

Benedick

Were you in doubt, sir, that you ask'd her?

100. ***have it full*** have your answer.
101–2. ***fathers herself*** resembles her father.

108. ***marks*** pays attention to.
109. ***Disdain*** contempt, scorn.
109. ***yet*** still.

111. ***meet*** appropriate.

114. ***turncoat*** traitor.

119. ***pernicious*** very harmful.
120. ***humour*** temperament.

124–5. ***scape a predestinate scratched face avoid an inevitable*** scratched face.

Leonato

Signior Benedick, no; for then were you a child.

Don Pedro

You have it full. Benedick; we may guess by this what you are, being a man. Truly, the lady fathers herself. Be happy, lady, for you are like an honourable father.

Benedick

If Signior Leonato be her father, she would not have his head on her shoulders for all Messina, as like him as she is.

Beatrice

I wonder that you will still be talking, Signior Benedick; nobody marks you.

Benedick

What, my dear Lady Disdain! Are you yet living?

Beatrice

Is it possible disdain should die while she hath such meet food to feed it as Signior Benedick? Courtesy itself must convert to disdain if you come in her presence.

Benedick

Then is courtesy a turncoat. But it is certain I am loved of all ladies, only you excepted; and I would I could find in my heart that I had not a hard heart, for, truly, I love none.

Beatrice

A dear happiness to women! They would else have been troubled with a pernicious suitor. I thank God, and my cold blood, I am of your humour for that: I had rather hear my dog bark at a crow than a man swear he loves me.

Benedick

God keep your ladyship still in that mind! So some gentleman or other shall scape a predestinate scratch'd face.

Beatrice

Scratching could not make it worse, an 'twere such a face as yours were.

128. ***parrot-teacher*** a repeater of meaningless words or phrases, 'parrot-fashion'.

131. ***so good a continuer*** could keep going for such a long time.

133. ***jade's trick*** getting out of the argument, like a poorly-trained horse that escapes its harness.

141. ***forsworn*** rejected, denied.

151. ***noted her not*** did not look at her that closely.

Benedick
Well, you are a a rare parrot-teacher.

Beatrice
A bird of my tongue is better than a beast of yours.

Benedick
I would my horse had the speed of your tongue, and so good a continuer. But keep your way a God's name, I have done.

Beatrice
You always end with a jade's trick; I know you of old.

Don Pedro
That is the sum of all, Leonato. Signior Claudio and Signior Benedick, my dear friend Leonato hath invited you all. I tell him we shall stay here at the least a month; and he heartily prays some occasion may detain us longer. I dare swear he is no hypocrite, but prays from his heart.

Leonato
If you swear, my lord, you shall not be forsworn. *[To* DON JOHN*]* Let me bid you welcome, my lord – being reconciled to the Prince your brother, I owe you all duty.

Don John
I thank you; I am not of many words, but I thank you.

Leonato
Please it your Grace lead on?

Don Pedro
Your hand, Leonato; we will go together.

[Exeunt all but BENEDICK *and* CLAUDIO.*]*

Claudio
Benedick, didst thou note the daughter of Signior Leonato?

Benedick
I noted her not, but I look'd on her.

152. ***modest*** sweet, virginal.

155. ***after my custom*** in my own personal way.
155. ***professed*** admitted.

158. ***methinks*** I think.
158. ***low*** short.
159. ***brown*** dark-skinned.
162. ***unhandsome*** unattractive.

164. ***in sport*** joking.

169. ***flouting*** Jack mocking rogue.
169–71. ***do you play . . . rare carpenter*** Cupid (the Roman god of love) was blind, and Vulcan (the god of fire) was a blacksmith – i.e. are you making a fool of Hero by praising qualities she does not have?
171–172. ***Key . . . go in the song*** suit your mood.

Claudio

Is she not a modest young lady?

Benedick

Do you question me, as an honest man should do, for my simple true judgment; or would you have me speak after my custom, as being a professed tyrant to their sex?

Claudio

No, I pray thee speak in sober judgment.

Benedick

Why, i' faith, methinks she's too low for a high praise, too brown for a fair praise, and too little for a great praise; only this commendation I can afford her, that were she other than she is, she were unhandsome, and being no other but as she is, I do not like her.

Claudio

Thou thinkest I am in sport; I pray thee tell me truly how thou lik'st her.

Benedick

Would you buy her, that you inquire after her?

Claudio

Can the world buy such a jewel?

Benedick

Yea, and a case to put it into. But speak you this with a sad brow, or do you play the flouting Jack, to tell us Cupid is a good hare-finder, and Vulcan a rare carpenter? Come, in what key shall a man take you to go in the song?

Claudio

In mine eye she is the sweetest lady that ever I look'd on.

Benedick

I can see yet without spectacles, and I see no such matter; there's her cousin, an she were not possess'd with a fury, exceeds her as much in beauty as the first of May doth the last of December. But I hope you have no intent to turn husband, have you?

183. ***wear his cap*** according to convention, a man whose wife was unfaithful to him grew horns on his forehead so a married man would have to wear a cap, or other hat, to cover his horns.
184. ***three score*** sixty.
186. ***yoke*** wooden bar used to harness oxen.
186. ***sigh away Sundays*** spend Sundays at home with your wife.

190. ***constrain*** force.

203. ***Amen*** so be it.

Claudio

I would scarce trust myself, though I had sworn the contrary, if Hero would be my wife.

Benedick

Is't come to this? In faith, hath not the world one man but he will wear his cap with suspicion? Shall I never see a bachelor of threescore again? Go to, i' faith; an thou wilt needs thrust thy neck into a yoke, wear the print of it, and sigh away Sundays. Look, Don Pedro is returned to seek you.

[Re-enter DON PEDRO.*]*

Don Pedro

What secret hath held you here, that you followed not to Leonato's?

Benedick

I would your Grace would constrain me to tell.

Don Pedro

I charge thee on thy allegiance.

Benedick

You hear, Count Claudio; I can be secret as a dumb man, I would have you think so; but on my allegiance, mark you this, on my allegiance – he is in love. With who? now that is your Grace's part. Mark how short his answer is: with Hero, Leonato's short daughter.

Claudio

If this were so, so were it utt'red.

Benedick

Like the old tale, my lord: 'It is not so, nor 'twas not so; but, indeed. God forbid it should be so!'

Claudio

If my passion change not shortly. God forbid it should be otherwise!

Don Pedro

Amen, if you love her; for the lady is very well worthy.

205. ***fetch me in*** trick me.

206. ***By my troth*** on my word.

214–5. ***die in it at the stake*** be burnt to death for what I believe.

216. ***obstinate*** stubborn.
216. ***heretic*** non-believer.
216. ***in the despite of beauty*** in scorning beauty.

222. ***recheat*** hunting call using a horn.
222. ***winded*** played.
223. ***bugle*** hunting horn.
223. ***baldrick*** belt for holding a bugle.

226. ***fine*** conclusion.

Claudio
You speak this to fetch me in, my lord?

Don Pedro
By my troth, I speak my thought.

Claudio
And, in faith, my lord, I spoke mine.

Benedick
And, by my two faiths and troths, my lord I spoke mine.

Claudio
That I love her, I feel.

Don Pedro
That she is worthy, I know.

Benedick
That I neither feel how she should be loved, nor know how she should be worthy, is the opinion that fire cannot melt out of me; I will die in it at the stake.

Don Pedro
Thou wast ever an obstinate heretic in the despite of beauty.

Claudio
And never could maintain his part but in the force of his will.

Benedick
That a woman conceived me, I thank her; that she brought me up, I likewise give her most humble thanks; but that I will have a recheat winded in my forehead, or hang my bugle in an invisible baldrick, all women shall pardon me. Because I will not do them the wrong to mistrust any, I will do myself the right to trust none; and the fine is, for the which I may go the finer, I will live a bachelor.

Don Pedro
I shall see thee, ere I die, look pale with love.

Benedick
With anger, with sickness, or with hunger, my lord; not with love. Prove that ever I lose more blood with

232. ***ballad-maker*** writer of romantic songs.
233–4. ***sign of blind Cupid*** brothel sign.

235. ***fall from this faith*** change your opinion.
236. ***argument*** subject for discussion.

237. ***bottle*** wicker basket.

239. ***Adam*** a celebrated archer of the time.

240. ***shall try*** will show.
240–1. ***In time the savage bull doth bear the yoke*** even a wild animal will be tamed in the end.

248–9. ***horn-mad*** raving mad.

250. ***spent all his quiver*** used up all his arrows.
251. ***Venice*** famous for loose morals.

253. ***temporise with the hours*** change as time passes.
254. ***repair*** go.

love than I will get again with drinking, pick out mine eyes with a ballad-maker's pen, and hang me up at the door of a brothel-house for the sign of blind Cupid.

Don Pedro

Well, if ever thou dost fall from this faith, thou wilt prove a notable argument.

Benedick

If I do, hang me in a bottle like a cat, and shoot at me; and he that hits me, let him be clapp'd on the shoulder and call'd Adam.

Don Pedro

Well, as time shall try. 'In time the savage bull doth bear the yoke.'

Benedick

The savage bull may; but if ever the sensible Benedick bear it, pluck off the bull's horns and set them in my forehead, and let me be vilely painted; and in such great letters as they write 'Here is good horse to hire' let them signify under my sign 'Here you may see Benedick the married man'.

Claudio

If this should ever happen, thou wouldst be horn-mad.

Don Pedro

Nay, if Cupid have not spent all his quiver in Venice, thou wilt quake for this shortly.

Benedick

I look for an earthquake too, then.

Don Pedro

Well, you will temporize with the hours. In the meantime, good Signior Benedick, repair to Leonato's; commend me to him, and tell him I will not fail him at supper; for, indeed, he hath made great preparation.

Benedick

I have almost matter enough in me for such an embassage; and so I commit you –

260. ***tuition*** protection.

263. ***discourse*** conversation.
263. ***guarded*** decorated or protected.
264. ***basted*** loosely sewn.
265. ***flout*** scoff or mock.

267. ***liege*** lord.

269. ***apt*** eager.

273. ***affect*** care for, love.

276. ***rougher task in hand*** more unpleasant job to do.

280. ***thronging*** swarming.

282. ***ere*** before.

Claudio
To the tuition of God. From my house – if I had it –

Don Pedro
The sixth of July. Your loving friend, Benedick.

Benedick
Nay, mock not, mock not. The body of your discourse is sometime guarded with fragments, and the guards are but slightly basted on neither; ere you flout old ends any further, examine your conscience; and so I leave you.

[*Exit* BENEDICK.]

Claudio
My liege, your Highness now may do me good.

Don Pedro
My love is thine to teach; teach it but how,
And thou shalt see how apt it is to learn
Any hard lesson that may do thee good.

Claudio
Hath Leonato any son, my lord?

Don Pedro
No child but Hero; she's his only heir.
Dost thou affect her, Claudio?

Claudio
O, my lord,
When you went onward on this ended action,
I look'd upon her with a soldier's eye,
That lik'd, but had a rougher task in hand
Than to drive liking to the name of love;
But now I am return'd, and that war-thoughts
Have left their places vacant, in their rooms
Come thronging soft and delicate desires,
All prompting me how fair young Hero is,
Saying I lik'd her ere I went to wars.

Don Pedro
Thou wilt be like a lover presently,
And tire the hearer with a book of words.
If thou dost love fair Hero, cherish it;

286. ***break with open discussion on the subject.***
287. ***to this end*** for this purpose.

290. ***complexion*** appearance.

292. ***salv'd it*** presented it more moderately.
292. ***treatise*** description.
293. ***What need the bridge much broader than the flood?*** a bridge only needs to be wide enough to cross the river.
294. ***The fairest grant is the necessity*** the best gift is one that meets the need.
295. ***'Tis once*** in a word.
296. ***fit*** provide.
297. ***revelling*** partying.
298. ***thy part*** your identity.
300. ***unclasp my heart*** reveal that I love her.

302. ***amorous*** showing love or desire.

And I will break with her, and with her father,
And thou shalt have her. Was't not to this end
That thou began'st to twist so fine a story?

Claudio

How sweetly you do minister to love,
That know love's grief by his complexion!
But lest my liking might too sudden seem,
I would have salv'd it with a longer treatise.

Don Pedro

What need the bridge much broader than the flood?
The fairest grant is the necessity.
Look what will serve is fit. 'Tis once, thou lovest;
And I will fit thee with the remedy.
I know we shall have revelling to-night;
I will assume thy part in some disguise,
And tell fair Hero I am Claudio;
And in her bosom I'll unclasp my heart,
And take her hearing prisoner with the force
And strong encounter of my amorous tale.
Then, after, to her father will I break;
And the conclusion is she shall be thine.
In practice let us put it presently.

[Exeunt.]

SCENE II

At first glance this may appear an unimportant scene, but it might be used to suggest the passing of time, the preparation for the party (hence the reference to 'this music'). Whilst the mistake made by Antonio has no real effect, it does hint at what's to come – more mistaken identity, and the idea of someone being 'overheard' or secretly observed is central to the play, as are the confusions that arise from it.

1. ***How now*** what news?
1. ***cousin*** family member.

6. ***As the event stamps them*** it depends on the outcome.
7. ***show well outward*** seem good.
8. ***thick-pleached*** heavily-covered with branches.

10. ***discovered*** revealed.

13. ***accordant*** agreeable.
13–14. ***take the present time by the top*** seize the moment/ opportunity.
14. ***break with you*** discuss it with you.
15. ***wit*** sense, intelligence.

18–19. ***till it appear itself*** until it actually happens.
19. ***acquaint*** inform.
19. ***withal*** as well.
21. ***peradventure*** by chance.

23. ***cry you mercy*** beg your pardon.
24. ***have a care*** be careful.

Scene II

Leonato's house.

[Enter, severally, LEONATO *and* ANTONIO.*]*

Leonato

How now, brother! Where is my cousin, your son? Hath he provided this music?

Antonio

He is very busy about it. But, brother, I can tell you strange news that you yet dreamt not of.

Leonato

Are they good?

Antonio

As the event stamps them; but they have a good cover; they show well outward. The Prince and Count Claudio, walking in a thick-pleached alley in mine orchard, were thus much overheard by a man of mine: the Prince discovered to Claudio that he loved my niece your daughter, and meant to acknowledge it this night in a dance; and, if he found her accordant, he meant to take the present time by the top, and instantly break with you of it.

Leonato

Hath the fellow any wit that told you this?

Antonio

A good sharp fellow; I will send for him, and question him yourself.

Leonato

No, no; we will hold it as a dream, till it appear itself; but I will acquaint my daughter withal, that she may be the better prepared for an answer, if peradventure this be true. Go you and tell her of it. *[Several persons cross the stage]* Cousins, you know what you have to do. O, I cry you mercy, friend; go with me, and I will use your skill. Good cousin, have a care this busy time.

[Exeunt.]

SCENE III

This important scene reveals how an otherwise light play, focused on love and wit, will have a darker side represented and given force by Don John's jealousy and bad humour. The scene itself sows the seeds for what will happen later when Don John says: '. . . if I can cross him (Claudio) any way, I bless myself . . .'. It is not completely clear why Don John acts in this way – Claudio hasn't actually done him any harm directly – except to spite the success and achievements of a younger and more popular rival. Note that the theme of disguise and the plot device of eavesdropping are both present in Borachio's hiding 'behind the arras' and overhearing the Prince's plans which parallels what Antonio's servant had heard (wrongly) earlier.

1. ***What the good year*** what on earth.

1–2. ***out of measure*** extremely.

7. ***remedy*** solution.

7. ***sufferance*** endurance.

9. ***born under Saturn*** sour and gloomy by nature.

9–10. ***moral medicine*** advice.

10. ***mortifying mischief*** deadly disease.

15. ***claw*** flatter.

18. ***stood out*** rebelled.

22. ***frame the season for your own harvest*** behave in a way that will benefit you.

23. ***canker*** wild rose, i.e. an outsider.

Scene III

Leonato's house.

[*Enter* DON JOHN *and* CONRADE.]

Conrade

What the good-year, my lord! Why are you thus out of measure sad?

Don John

There is no measure in the occasion that breeds; therefore the sadness is without limit.

Conrade

You should hear reason.

Don John

And when I have heard it, what blessing brings it?

Conrade

If not a present remedy, at least a patient sufferance.

Don John

I wonder that thou, being, as thou say'st thou art, born under Saturn, goest about to apply a moral medicine to a mortifying mischief. I cannot hide what I am; I must be sad when I have cause, and smile at no man's jests; eat when I have stomach, and wait for no man's leisure; sleep when I am drowsy, and tend on no man's business; laugh when I am merry, and claw no man in his humour.

Conrade

Yea, but you must not make the full show of this till you may do it without controlment. You have of late stood out against your brother, and he hath ta'en you newly into his grace; where it is impossible you should take true root but by the fair weather that you make yourself; it is needful that you frame the season for your own harvest.

Don John

I had rather be a canker in a hedge than a rose in his grace; and it better fits my blood to be disdain'd of

25. ***fashion a carriage*** put on an act, pretend to be something I am not.

29. ***muzzle*** strap over an animal's jaws to prevent it biting.
29. ***clog*** wooden block fitted to an animal's leg.

35. ***use it only*** it is my only means.

41. ***model*** plan.
42. ***betroths*** becomes engaged.
43. ***unquietness*** noise, but here meaning conflict and 'disquiet' (in marriage).
44. ***Marry*** by the Virgin Mary.

47. ***squire*** nobleman.

50. ***forward March-chick*** precocious youngster.

all than to fashion a carriage to rob love from any. In this, though I cannot be said to be a flattering honest man, it must not be denied but I am a plain-dealing villain. I am trusted with a muzzle and enfranchis'd with a clog; therefore I have decreed not to sing in my cage. If I had my mouth, I would bite; if I had my liberty, I would do my liking; in the meantime let me be that I am, and seek not to alter me.

Conrade

Can you make no use of your discontent?

Don John

I make all use of it, for I use it only. Who comes here?

[*Enter* BORACHIO.]

What news, Borachio?

Borachio

I came yonder from a great supper. The Prince, your brother, is royally entertain'd by Leonato; and I can give you intelligence of an intended marriage.

Don John

Will it serve for any model to build mischief on? What is he for a fool that betroths himself to unquietness?

Borachio

Marry, it is your brother's right hand.

Don John

Who? The most exquisite Claudio?

Borachio

Even he.

Don John

A proper squire! And who, and who? Which way looks he?

Borachio

Marry, on Hero, the daughter and heir of Leonato.

Don John

A very forward March-chick! How came you to this?

51. ***entertained for*** hired as.
51. ***smoking*** fumigating.
53. ***sad*** serious.
54. ***arras*** wall-hanging or curtain.

57. ***thither*** there.
58. ***start-up*** upstart.

60. ***sure*** loyal.

64–5. ***o' my mind thought as I do,*** i.e. to poison the guests.
65. ***prove*** find out, discover.

Borachio

Being entertain'd for a perfumer, as I was smoking a musty room, comes me the Prince and Claudio hand in hand, in sad conference. I whipt me behind the arras, and there heard it agreed upon that the Prince should woo Hero for himself, and, having obtain'd her, give her to Count Claudio.

Don John

Come, come, let us thither; this may prove food to my displeasure; that young start-up hath all the glory of my overthrow. If I can cross him any way, I bless myself every way. You are both sure, and will assist me?

Conrade

To the death, my lord.

Don John

Let us to the great supper; their cheer is the greater that I am subdued. Would the cook were o' my mind! Shall we go prove what's to be done?

Borachio

We'll wait upon your lordship.

[Exeunt.]

ACT II SCENE I

Full of misunderstandings, jokes, the battle of the sexes, and interweaving the themes of disguise, marriage negotiation and love, this long scene is important because it sets the tone for the play. As Beatrice says, 'wooing, wedding, and repenting, is as a Scotch jig.' Here, she links the process of love and marriage, with a type of dance (a jig) – and this fits the play and scene perfectly. Masks are put on, people come and go, and the audience hears one quick conversation, then another. It is fast paced and lively – like the jig. Everyone – at some point or other – wears a mask, reminding us not only of the importance of physical disguise to the story of the play, but also of inner deceptions – pretending to be something you are not.

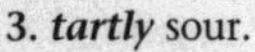

3. ***tartly*** sour.

5. ***melancholy disposition*** morose and negative character.

8. ***image*** statue.
9. ***tattling*** talking.

15. ***if 'a could*** if he could.

17. ***shrewd*** sharp.

19. ***curst*** bad-tempered.

ACT TWO

Scene I

A hall in Leonato's house.

[Enter LEONATO, ANTONIO, HERO, BEATRICE, MARGARET, URSULA, *and* OTHERS.*]*

Leonato
Was not Count John here at supper?

Antonio
I saw him not.

Beatrice
How tartly that gentleman looks! I never can see him but I am heart-burn'd an hour after.

Hero
He is of a very melancholy disposition.

Beatrice
He were an excellent man that were made just in the mid-way between him and Benedick: the one is too like an image and says nothing, and the other too like my lady's eldest son, evermore tattling.

Leonato
Then half Signior Benedick's tongue in Count John's mouth, and half Count John's melancholy in Signior Benedick's face –

Beatrice
With a good leg and a good foot, uncle, and money enough in his purse, such a man would win any woman in the world, if 'a could get her good-will.

Leonato
By my troth, niece, thou wilt never get thee a husband if thou be so shrewd of thy tongue.

Antonio
In faith, she's too curst.

Beatrice
Too curst is more than curst. I shall lessen

20. ***God's sending*** what God has given me.
20–21. ***God sends a curst cow short horns*** God prevents vicious people in doing damage to others.

24. ***Just*** exactly.

27–8. ***in the woollen*** on coarse, rough blankets.

31. ***apparel*** clothes.

36. ***earnest*** payment in advance.
36. ***berrord*** bear-keeper.

40. ***cuckold*** man with an unfaithful wife.

43. ***Saint Peter*** guardian of the gates of heaven.

God's sending that way; for it is said 'God sends a curst cow short horns'; but to a cow too curst he sends none.

Leonato

So, by being too curst. God will send you no horns.

Beatrice

Just, if he send me no husband; for the which blessing I am at him upon my knees every morning and evening. Lord! I could not endure a husband with a beard on is face; I had rather lie in the woollen.

Leonato

You may light on a husband that hath no beard.

Beatrice

What should I do with him? Dress him in my apparel, and make him my waiting gentlewoman? He that hath a beard is more than a youth, and he that hath no beard is less than a man; and he that is more than a youth is not for me, and he that is less than a man I am not for him; therefore I will even take sixpence in earnest of the berrord, and lead his apes into hell.

Leonato

Well then, go you into hell?

Beatrice

No; but to the gate, and there will the devil meet me, like an old cuckold, with horns on his head, and say 'Get you to heaven, Beatrice, get you to heaven; here's no place for you maids'. So deliver I up my apes and away to Saint Peter for the heavens; he shows me where the bachelors sit, and there live we as merry as the day is long.

Antonio

[To HERO*]* Well, niece, I trust you will be rul'd by your father.

Beatrice

Yes, faith; it is my cousin's duty to make curtsy, and

54. ***metal*** material.

56. ***dust*** refers to the idea that God created the first man, Adam, from dust.
57. ***marl*** clay.
58. ***brethren*** brothers.
59. ***match in my kindred*** marry a close relative.

61. ***in that kind*** for that reason (i.e to propose marriage).

63. ***important*** hasty.
64. ***measure*** moderation, also a dignified dance.

67. ***cinquepace*** a lively, vivacious dance.
67. ***first suit*** wooing.

70. ***ancientry*** polite etiquette.

73. ***passing shrewdly*** very sharply.

say 'Father, as it please you'. But yet for all that, cousin, let him be a handsome fellow, or else make another curtsy and say 'Father, as it please me.'

Leonato

Well, niece, I hope to see you one day fitted with a husband.

Beatrice

Not till God make men of some other metal than earth. Would it not grieve a woman to be over-master'd with a piece of valiant dust, to make an account of her life to a clod of wayward marl? No, uncle, I'll none: Adam's sons are my brethren; and, truly, I hold it a sin to match in my kindred.

Leonato

Daughter, remember what I told you: if the Prince do solicit you in that kind, you know your answer.

Beatrice

The fault will be in the music, cousin, if you be not wooed in good time. If the Prince be too important, tell him there is measure in every thing, and so dance out the answer. For, hear me, Hero: wooing, wedding, and repenting, is as a Scotch jig, a measure, and a cinquepace; the first suit is hot and hasty, like a Scotch jig, and full as fantastical; the wedding, mannerly modest, as a measure, full of state and ancientry; and then comes repentance, and, with his bad legs, falls into the cinquepace faster and faster, till he sink into his grave.

Leonato

Cousin, you apprehend passing shrewdly.

Beatrice

I have a good eye, uncle; I can see a church by daylight.

Leonato

The revellers are ent'ring, brother; make good room.

[ANTONIO *masks.]*

[Enter DON PEDRO, CLAUDIO, BENEDICK, BALTHASAR, DON JOHN, *and* BORACHIO, *as maskers, with a drum.]*

77. ***walk about*** dance.

78. ***So you*** if you.

84. ***favour*** face.
84. ***defend*** forbid.

86. ***visor*** mask.
86. ***Philemon*** in myth, a poor peasant who gave Jove shelter, unaware who he was.
87. ***Jove*** king of the Roman gods.

92. ***ill qualities*** poor, unpleasant characteristics.

95. ***Amen*** so be it.

Don Pedro
Lady, will you walk about with your friend?

Hero
So you walk softly, and look sweetly, and say nothing, I am yours for the walk; and, especially, when I walk away.

Don Pedro
With me in your company?

Hero
I may say so, when I please.

Don Pedro
And when please you to say so?

Hero
When I like your favour; for God defend the lute should be like the case!

Don Pedro
My visor is Philemon's roof; within the house is Jove.

Hero
Why, then, your visor should be thatch'd.

Don Pedro
Speak low, if you speak love.

[Takes her aside.]

Balthasar
Well, I would you did like me.

Margaret
So would not I, for your own sake; for I have many ill qualities.

Balthasar
Which is one?

Margaret
I say my prayers aloud.

Balthasar
I love you the better; the hearers may cry Amen.

Margaret
God match me with a good dancer!

100. ***clerk*** church official who leads the prayer responses.

104. ***counterfeit*** imitate, fake.

106. ***up and down*** entirely.

111. ***mum*** be silent.

118. ***Hundred Merry Tales*** a collection of humorous stories.

Balthasar

Amen.

Margaret

And God keep him out of my sight when the dance is done! Answer, clerk.

Balthasar

No more words; the clerk is answered.

Ursula

I know you well enough; you are Signior Antonio.

Antonio

At a word, I am not.

Ursula

I know you by the waggling of your head.

Antonio

To tell you true, I counterfeit him.

Ursula

You could never do him so ill-well unless you were the very man. Here's his dry hand up and down; you are he, you are he.

Antonio

At a word, I am not.

Ursula

Come, come; do you think I do not know you by your excellent wit? Can virtue hide itself? Go to; mum; you are he; graces will appear, and there's an end.

Beatrice

Will you not tell me who told you so?

Benedick

No, you shall pardon me.

Beatrice

Nor will you not tell me who you are?

Benedick

Not now.

Beatrice

That I was disdainful, and that I had my good wit out of the 'Hundred Merry Tales' – well, this was Signior Benedick that said so.

120. ***what is he*** who is he.

125–6. ***only his gift*** his only talent.
127. ***libertines*** immoral people.
128. ***villainy*** offensiveness.

130. ***fleet*** company.
131. ***boarded*** tackled.

134. ***break a comparison or two on me*** mock me with one or two witty remarks.
135. ***mark'd*** paid attention to.

142. ***amorous on*** in love with.

Benedick
What's he?

Beatrice
I am sure you know him well enough.

Benedick
Not I, believe me.

Beatrice
Did he never make you laugh?

Benedick
I pray you, what is he?

Beatrice
Why, he is the Prince's jester, a very dull fool; only his gift is in devising impossible slanders; none but libertines delight in him, and the commendation is not in his wit but in his villainy; for he both pleases men and angers them, and then they laugh at him and beat him. I am sure he is in the fleet; I would he had boarded me.

Benedick
When I know the gentleman, I'll tell him what you say.

Beatrice
Do, do; he'll but break a comparison or two on me; which, peradventure, not mark'd, or not laugh'd at, strikes him into melancholy; and then there's a partridge wing saved, for the fool will eat no supper that night. *[Music]* We must follow the leaders.

Benedick
In every good thing.

Beatrice
Nay, if they lead to any ill, I will leave them at the next turning.

[Dance. Then exeunt all but DON JOHN, BORACHIO, *and* CLAUDIO.*]*

Don John
Sure, my brother is amorous on Hero, and hath withdrawn her father to break with him about it.

145. ***bearing*** manner.

149. ***enamour'd on*** in love with.

165. ***faith*** loyalty.
165. ***blood*** desire.
166. ***accident of hourly proof*** something which is shown to be true every hour.
167. ***mistrusted not*** did not suspect.

The ladies follow her, and but one visor remains.

Borachio

And that is Claudio; I know him by his bearing.

Don John

Are not you Signior Benedick?

Claudio

You know me well; I am he.

Don John

Signior, you are very near my brother in his love; he is enamour'd on Hero; I pray you dissuade him from her; she is no equal for his birth. You may do the part of an honest man in it.

Claudio

How know you he loves her?

Don John

I heard him swear his affection.

Borachio

So did I too; and he swore he would marry her tonight.

Don John

Come, let us to the banquet.

[*Exeunt* DON JOHN *and* BORACHIO.]

Claudio

Thus answer I in name of Benedick,
But hear these ill news with the ears of Claudio.
'Tis certain so: the Prince woos for himself.
Friendship is constant in all other things
Save in the office and affairs of love;
Therefore all hearts in love use their own tongues.
Let every eye negotiate for itself.
And trust no agent; for beauty is a witch
Against whose charms faith melteth into blood.
This is an accident of hourly proof,
Which I mistrusted not. Farewell, therefore, Hero.

[*Re-enter* BENEDICK.]

170. ***Whither*** where.

172. ***County*** count.
172. ***garland*** a willow garland was the symbol of a rejected lover.
173. ***usurer's chain*** a money-lender's necklace.
174. ***lieutenant's scarf*** soldier's sash.

177. ***drovier*** cattle-seller.

179. ***served you thus*** treated you like this.

184. ***hurt fowl*** game bird that has been shot down.
184. ***sedges*** undergrowth.

189. ***base*** dishonourable.
189–90. ***puts the world into her person*** assumes everyone thinks in the way she does.
190. ***gives me out*** says such things about me.

Benedick
Count Claudio?

Claudio
Yea, the same.

Benedick
Come, will you go with me?

Claudio
Whither?

Benedick
Even to the next willow, about your own business, County. What fashion will you wear the garland of? About your neck, like an usurer's chain, or under your arm, like a lieutenant's scarf? You must wear it one way, for the Prince hath got your Hero.

Claudio
I wish him joy other.

Benedick
Why, that's spoken like an honest drovier; so they sell bullocks. But did you think the Prince would have served you thus?

Claudio
I pray you leave me.

Benedick
Ho! now you strike like the blind man; 'twas the boy that stole your meat, and you'll beat the post.

Claudio
If it will not be, I'll leave you.

[Exit.]

Benedick
Alas, poor hurt fowl! Now will he creep into sedges. But that my Lady Beatrice should know me, and not know me! The Prince's fool! Ha! It may be I go under that title because I am merry. Yea, but so I am apt to do myself wrong; I am not so reputed; it is the base, though bitter, disposition of Beatrice that puts the world into her person, and so gives me out. Well, I'll be revenged as I may.

193. ***Troth*** truly.
193. ***Lady Fame*** Rumour (personified here).
194–5. ***lodge in a warren*** a hut (possibly a gamekeeper's) in a hunting area.

201. ***flat transgression*** blatant rule-breaking.

206. ***amiss*** for no purpose.

Re-enter DON PEDRO.

Don Pedro
Now, signior, where's the Count? Did you see him?

Benedick
Troth, my lord, I have played the part of Lady Fame. I found him here as melancholy as a lodge in a warren; I told him, and I think I told him true, that your Grace had got the good will of this young lady; and I off'red him my company to a willow tree, either to make him a garland, as being forsaken, or to bind him up a rod, as being worthy to be whipt.

Don Pedro
To be whipt! What's his fault?

Benedick
The flat transgression of a schoolboy, who, being overjoyed with finding a bird's nest, shows it his companion, and he steals it.

Don Pedro
Wilt thou make a trust a transgression? The transgression is in the stealer.

Benedick
Yet it had not been amiss the rod had been made, and the garland too; for the garland he might have worn himself, and the rod he might have bestowed on you, who, as I take it, have stol'n his bird's nest.

Don Pedro
I will but teach them to sing, and restore them to the owner.

Benedick
If their singing answer your saying, by my faith, you say honestly.

Don Pedro
The Lady Beatrice hath a quarrel to you; the gentleman that danc'd with her told her she is much wrong'd by you.

Benedick
O, she misus'd me past the endurance of a block; an

219. ***my very visor*** even my mask.

222. ***duller than a great thaw*** more boring than being stuck at home when the roads are impassable due to mud.
223. ***impossible conveyance*** incredible skill.
225. ***poniards*** daggers.

227. ***terminations*** ways of describing someone (like 'terms').

229–30. ***all that Adam had left him before he transgress'd*** Adam had power over all creation until he disobeyed God.
231. ***made Hercules have turn'd spit*** forced Hercules (a symbol of masculinity) to turn the roasting spit, i.e. perform women's work.
233. ***Ate*** goddess of discord.
233. ***good apparel*** seeming good on the outside ('apparel' means clothing).
234. ***scholar*** someone who could perform exorcisms.

242. ***Antipodes*** the other side of the world.
242. ***devise*** think of.
244. ***Prester John*** a legendary Christian king.
245. ***great Cham*** emperor of the Mongols.
246. ***embassage*** errand.
247. ***harpy*** mythical monster with a woman's face, but bird's wings and claws.

oak but with one green leaf on it would have answered her; my very visor began to assume life and scold with her. She told me, not thinking I had been myself, that I was the Prince's jester, that I was duller than a great thaw; huddling jest upon jest with such impossible conveyance upon me that I stood like a man at a mark, with a whole army shooting at me. She speaks poniards, and every word stabs; if her breath were as terrible as her terminations, there were no living near her; she would infect to the north star. I would not marry her though she were endowed with all that Adam had left him before he transgress'd; she would have made Hercules have turn'd spit, yea, and have cleft his club to make the fire too. Come, talk not of her; you shall find her the infernal Ate in good apparel. I would to God some scholar would conjure her; for certainly, while she is here, a man may live as quiet in hell as in a sanctuary; and people sin upon purpose, because they would go thither; so, indeed, all disquiet, horror, and perturbation, follows her.

[Re-enter CLAUDIO *and* BEATRICE, LEONATO *and* HERO.*]*

Don Pedro

Look, here she comes.

Benedick

Will your Grace command me any service to the world's end? I will go on the slightest errand now to the Antipodes that you can devise to send me on; I will fetch you a toothpicker now from the furthest inch of Asia; bring you the length of Prester John's foot; fetch you a hair off the great Cham's beard; do you any embassage to the Pigmies – rather than hold three words' conference with this harpy. You have no employment for me?

Don Pedro

None, but to desire your good company.

258. ***put him down*** put him in his place (with your comments). Beatrice chooses to take these words to have a ruder meaning, saying she wouldn't want Benedick to put her down (i.e on a bed!).

268. ***civil as an orange*** there is a play on words here; probably on a Seville ('civil') orange; it is interesting to note the use of the word 'orange' in a much less humorous context later when Claudio calls Hero a 'rotten orange.'
270. ***blazon*** description.
271. ***conceit*** idea.

Benedick

O God, sir, here's a dish I love not; I cannot endure my Lady Tongue.

[Exit.]

Don Pedro

Come, lady, come; you have lost the heart of Signior Benedick.

Beatrice

Indeed, my lord, he lent it me awhile; and I gave him use for it, a double heart for his single one; marry, once before he won it of me with false dice, therefore your Grace may well say I have lost it.

Don Pedro

You have put him down, lady, you have put him down.

Beatrice

So I would not he should do me, my lord, lest I should prove the mother of fools. I have brought Count Claudio, whom you sent me to seek.

Don Pedro

Why, how now, Count! Wherefore are you sad?

Claudio

Not sad, my lord.

Don Pedro

How then, sick?

Claudio

Neither, my lord.

Beatrice

The Count is neither sad, nor sick, nor merry, nor well; but civil count – civil as an orange, and something of that jealous complexion.

Don Pedro

I' faith, lady, I think your blazon to be true, though I'll be sworn, if he be so, his conceit is false. Here, Claudio, I have wooed in thy name, and fair Hero is won. I have broke with her father, and his good will

284. ***stop*** fill, cover.

287–8. ***on the windy side of in the best,*** safest place.

291. ***alliance*** such togetherness.
291–2. ***goes every one to the world*** gets married.
292. ***sunburnt*** means unattractive in this context.

295. ***getting*** fathering (similar to 'beget').

obtained. Name the day of marriage, and God give thee joy!

Leonato

Count, take of me my daughter, and with her my fortunes; his Grace hath made the match, and all grace say Amen to it!

Beatrice

Speak, Count, 'tis your cue.

Claudio

Silence is the perfectest herald of joy: I were but little happy if I could say how much. Lady, as you are mine, I am yours; I give away myself for you, and dote upon the exchange.

Beatrice

Speak, cousin; or, if you cannot, stop his mouth with a kiss, and let not him speak neither.

Don Pedro

In faith, lady, you have a merry heart.

Beatrice

Yea, my lord; I thank it, poor fool, it keeps on the windy side of care. My cousin tells him in his ear that he is in her heart.

Claudio

And so she doth, cousin.

Beatrice

Good Lord, for alliance! Thus goes every one to the world but I, and I am sunburnt; I may sit in a corner and cry 'Heigh-ho for a husband!'

Don Pedro

Lady Beatrice, I will get you one.

Beatrice

I would rather have one of your father's getting. Hath your Grace ne'er a brother like you? Your father got excellent husbands, if a maid could come by them.

Don Pedro

Will you have me, lady?

303. ***mirth*** jokes.

303. ***no matter*** nothing serious.

305. ***becomes*** suits.

311. ***cry you mercy*** apologise.

315. ***ever*** always.

318–9. ***out of suit*** out of pursuing her.

Beatrice

No, my lord, unless I might have another for working-days; your Grace is too costly to wear every day. But, I beseech your Grace, pardon me; I was bom to speak all mirth and no matter.

Don Pedro

Your silence most offends me, and to be merry best becomes you; for, out o' question, you were born in a merry hour.

Beatrice

No, sure, my lord, my mother cried; but then there was a star danc'd, and under that was I born. Cousins, God give you joy!

Leonato

Niece, you will look to those things I told you of?

Beatrice

I cry your mercy, uncle. By your Grace's pardon.

[*Exit* BEATRICE.]

Don Pedro

By my troth, a pleasant-spirited lady.

Leonato

There's little of the melancholy element in her, my lord; she is never sad but when she sleeps, and not ever sad then; for I have heard my daughter say she hath often dreamt of unhappiness, and wak'd herself with laughing.

Don Pedro

She cannot endure to hear tell of a husband.

Leonato

O, by no means; she mocks all her wooers out of suit.

Don Pedro

She were an excellent wife for Benedick.

Leonato

O Lord, my lord, if they were but a week married, they would talk themselves mad.

326–7. ***a just seven-night*** exactly a week.
328. ***answer my mind*** arranged as I want them.

329. ***breathing*** wait.

331. ***interim*** meantime.
332. ***Hercules' labours*** tasks requiring tremendous effort or strength.

334. ***fain*** gladly.

336. ***minister*** provide.

339. ***watchings*** sleepless nights.

342. ***office*** task.

346. ***strain*** background and character.
346. ***approved valour*** proven bravery.
346–7. ***confirm'd honesty*** proven worthiness.

349. ***practise on*** work on.
350–1. ***queasy stomach*** distaste, lack of appetite (for marriage).

Don Pedro

County Claudio, when mean you to go to church?

Claudio

To-morrow, my lord. Time goes on crutches till love have all his rites.

Leonato

Not till Monday, my dear son, which is hence a just seven-night; and a time too brief, too, to have all things answer my mind.

Don Pedro

Come, you shake the head at so long a breathing; but I warrant thee, Claudio, the time shall not go dully by us. I will in the interim undertake one of Hercules' labours; which is, to bring Signior Benedick and the Lady Beatrice into a mountain of affection th' one with th' other. I would fain have it a match; and I doubt not but to fashion it if you three will but minister such assistance as I shall give you direction.

Leonato

My lord, I am for you, though it cost me ten nights' watchings.

Claudio

And I, my lord.

Don Pedro

And you too, gentle Hero?

Hero

I will do any modest office, my lord, to help my cousin to a good husband.

Don Pedro

And Benedick is not the unhopefullest husband that I know. Thus far can I praise him; he is of a noble strain, of approved valour, and confirm'd honesty. I will teach you how to humour your cousin that she shall fall in love with Benedick; and I, with your two helps, will so practise on Benedick that, in despite of his quick wit and his queasy stomach, he shall fall in love with Beatrice. If we can do this, Cupid is no

352. ***Cupid*** Roman god of love, who used a bow and arrow to shoot love at his 'victims'.

longer an archer; his glory shall be ours, for we are the only love-gods. Join with me, and I will tell you my drift.

[Exeunt.]

SCENE II

This brief scene follows hot on the heels of the last, and provides a parallel to what has just happened. Whereas Don Pedro's plans are to create joy – and love (between Beatrice and Benedick), Don John's and Borachio's are to create sorrow and mischief. What other parallel scenes occur in the play? (Think of the marriages, tricks, and so on.)

5. ***med'cinable*** soothing.
6. ***athwart*** his affection gets in the way of what he wants.
6–7. ***ranges evenly with mine*** pleases me.

16. ***unseasonable*** inappropriate.

20. ***temper*** mix.

24. ***stale*** prostitute.

Scene II

Leonato's house.

[Enter DON JOHN *and* BORACHIO.*]*

Don John

It is so: the Count Claudio shall marry the daughter of Leonato.

Borachio

Yea, my lord, but I can cross it.

Don John

Any bar, any cross, any impediment, will be med'cinable to me. I am sick in displeasure to him; and whatsoever comes athwart his affection ranges evenly with mine.How canst thou cross this marriage?

Borachio

Not honestly, my lord; but so covertly that no dishonesty shall appear in me.

Don John

Show me briefly how.

Borachio

I think I told your lordship a year since how much I am in the favour of Margaret, the waiting gentlewoman to Hero.

Don John

I remember.

Borachio

I can at any unseasonable instant of the night appoint her to look out at her lady's chamber window.

Don John

What life is in that, to be the death of this marriage?

Borachio

The poison of that lies in you to temper. Go you to the Prince your brother; spare not to tell him that he hath wronged his honour in marrying the renowned Claudio – whose estimation do you

27. ***misuse*** deceive or mislead.
27. ***vex*** distress, upset (someone).
29. ***issue*** result.

31. ***meet*** suitable.

33. ***intend*** put on.

37. ***cozen'd*** cheated.
37. ***semblance*** mock appearance (to deceive).
37. ***maid*** virgin.

42. ***term*** name.

44. ***fashion*** arrange.

50. ***ducats*** gold or silver coins of Italy.

mightily hold up – to a contaminated stale, such a one as Hero.

Don John

What proof shall I make of that?

Borachio

Proof enough to misuse the Prince, to vex Claudio, to undo Hero, and kill Leonato. Look you for any other issue?

Don John

Only to despite them I will endeavour anything.

Borachio

Go, then; find me a meet hour to draw Don Pedro and the Count Claudio alone; tell them that you know that Hero loves me; intend a kind of zeal both to the Prince and Claudio – as in love of your brother's honour, who hath made this match, and his friend's reputation, who is thus like to be cozen'd with the semblance of a maid – that you have discover'd thus. They will scarcely believe this without trial; offer them instances; which shall bear no less likelihood than to see me at her chamber window; hear me call Margaret Hero; hear Margaret term me Borachio; and bring them to see this the very night before the intended wedding – for in the meantime I will so fashion the matter that Hero shall be absent – and there shall appear such seeming truth of Hero's disloyalty that jealousy shall be call'd assurance, and all the preparation overthrown.

Don John

Grow this to what adverse issue it can, I will put it in practice. Be cunning in the working this, and thy fee is a thousand ducats.

Borachio

Be you constant in the accusation, and my cunning shall not shame me.

Don John

I will presently go learn their day of marriage.

[Exeunt.]

SCENE III

This scene signals the beginning of Benedick's transformation. Perhaps the seeds have been sown in Scene 1, but it is here that his love for Beatrice first shows itself. Don Pedro, Leonato, and Claudio's plot to bring Benedick and Beatrice together is especially clever because they pretend to be amazed, too, by Beatrice's love for him. As Don Pedro says (to Claudio). 'You amaze me: I would have thought her spirit had been invincible against all assaults of affection.' Of course, the whole scene is a plot to trap Benedick – at one point Claudio even says, 'Bait the hook well: this fish will bite', and Benedick certainly does!

10. ***follies*** foolish acts or behaviour.
11. ***argument*** object.

13–14. ***the drum and the fife*** musical instruments used in war.
14–15. ***the tabor and the pipe*** musical instruments for festivities.

17. ***carving*** designing.
18. ***doublet*** upper part of a man's outfit.
20. ***turn'd orthography*** speaking in flowery language.

24. ***transform me to an oyster*** shut me up like a clam.

Scene III

Leonato's orchard.

Enter BENEDICK, *alone.*

Benedick

Boy!

Boy

[Within] Signior?

Benedick

In my chamber-window lies a book; bring it hither to me in the orchard.

Boy

[Above, at chamber window] I am here already, sir.

Benedick

I know that; but I would have thee hence and here again. *[Boy brings book; Exit]* I do much wonder that one man, seeing how much another man is a fool when he dedicates his behaviours to love, will, after he hath laugh'd at such shallow follies in others, become the argument of his own scorn by falling in love; and such a man is Claudio. I have known when there was no music with him but the drum and the fife, and now had he rather hear the tabor and the pipe; I have known when he would have walk'd ten mile afoot to see a good armour, and now will he lie ten nights awake carving the fashion of a new doublet. He was wont to speak plain and to the purpose, like an honest man and a soldier, and now is he turn'd orthography; his words are a very fantastical banquet, just so many strange dishes. May I be so converted, and see with these eyes? I cannot tell; I think not. I will not be sworn but love may transform me to an oyster; but I'll take my oath on it, till he have made an oyster of me he shall never make me such a fool. One woman is fair, yet I am well; another is wise, yet I am well; another virtuous, yet I am well; but till all graces be in one woman, one

31. ***cheapen*** bargain for.
32–3. ***noble, angel*** types of coin, the first worth less than the second.
33. ***discourse*** conversation.

36. ***arbour*** garden shelter.

42. ***fit the kid-fox with a pennyworth*** give the lad more than he bargained for.

45. ***slander*** bring disgrace on.
46. ***witness*** sign.
47. ***strange*** surprised.

woman shall not come in my grace. Rich she shall be, that's certain; wise, or I'll none; virtuous, or I'll never cheapen her; fair, or I'll never look on her; mild, or come not near me; noble, or not I for an angel; of good discourse, an excellent musician, and her hair shall be of what colour it please God. Ha! the Prince and Monsieur Love! I will hide me in the arbour.

[Withdraws.]

[Enter DON PEDRO, LEONATO, *and* CLAUDIO.*]*

Don Pedro
Come, shall we hear this music?

Claudio
Yea, my good lord. How still the evening is,
As hush'd on purpose to grace harmony!

Don Pedro
See you where Benedick hath hid himself?

Claudio
O, very well, my lord; the music ended,
We'll fit the kid-fox with a pennyworth.

[Enter BALTHASAR, *with music.]*

Don Pedro
Come, Balthasar, we'll hear that song again.

Balthasar
O, good my lord, tax not so bad a voice
To slander music any more than once.

Don Pedro
It is the witness still of excellency
To put a strange face on his own perfection.
I pray thee sing, and let me woo no more.

Balthasar
Because you talk of wooing, I will sing,
Since many a wooer doth commence his suit
To her he thinks not worthy; yet he woos;
Yet will he swear he loves.

54. ***in notes*** briefly.

54. ***Note this before my notes . . .*** Listen to this before I sing/play. Balthasar's playing with the idea of music, watching ('noting') reminds us of the title of the play and its many meanings. Its ironic that Balthasar, who makes a joke about his own 'notes' (musical ones) then starts to sing!
56. ***crotchets*** musical notes, and whimsical ideas.

58. ***air*** music.
59. ***sheep's guts*** strings of a musical instrument.
59. ***hale*** summon.
60. ***horn*** hunting horn.

63. ***Men were deceivers ever*** Men have always been untrustworthy Balthasar's words have double irony in that Benedick is being deceived by other men (Pedro, Claudio and Leonato), but also hints at Don John's more sinister deception to come.
67. ***blithe and bonny*** cheerful and pretty.
68. ***woe*** sadness.

70. ***ditties*** songs.
70. ***moe*** more.
71. ***dumps*** sad mood or song (we say 'down in the dumps' meaning fed-up).

76. ***ill*** bad.

Don Pedro

Nay, pray thee, come;
Or if thou wilt hold longer argument,
Do it in notes.

Balthasar

Note this before my notes:
There's not a note of mine that's worth the noting.

Don Pedro

Why, these are very crotchets that he speaks;
Note notes, forsooth, and nothing!

[Music.]

Benedick

Now, divine air! now is his soul ravish'd. Is it not strange that sheeps' guts should hale souls out of men's bodies? Well, a horn for my money, when all's done.

[BALTHASAR *sings.]*

Sigh no more, ladies, sigh no more,
Men were deceivers ever,
One foot in sea and one on shore,
To one thing constant never.
Then sigh not so, but let them go,
And be you blithe and bonny;
Converting all your sounds of woe
Into Hey nonny nonny.
Sing no more ditties, sing no moe
Of dumps so dull and heavy;
The fraud of men was ever so,
Since summer first was leavy.
Then sigh not so, etc.

Don Pedro

By my troth, a good song.

Balthasar

And an ill singer, my lord.

77–8. ***for a shift*** as a last resort (i.e. having no other choice).

79. ***An*** if.

81. ***bode*** foretells.
81. ***as lief*** rather.
82. ***night-raven*** a croaking bird seen as a sign of disaster to come.
82. ***plague*** sickness.

93. ***stalk on, stalk on, the fowl sits*** move carefully, the game bird has settled in one spot.

97. ***abhor*** hate.
98. ***Sits the wind in that corner?*** Is that really how things are?

101. ***past the infinite of thought*** beyond understanding.
102. ***counterfeit*** pretend.

Claudio

Ha, no; no, faith; thou sing'st well enough for a shift.

Benedick

An he had been a dog that should have howl'd thus, they would have hang'd him; and I pray God his bad voice bode no mischief. I had as lief have heard the night-raven, come what plague could have come after it.

Don Pedro

Yea, marry; dost thou hear, Balthasar? I pray thee get us some excellent music; for to-morrow night we would have it at the Lady Hero's chamber window.

Balthasar

The best I can, my lord.

Don Pedro

Do so; farewell.

[*Exit* BALTHASAR.]

Come hither, Leonato. What was it you told me of to-day – that your niece Beatrice was in love with Signior Benedick?

Claudio

O ay; stalk on, stalk on; the fowl sits. I did never think that lady would have loved any man.

Leonato

No, nor I neither; but most wonderful that she should so dote on Signior Benedick, whom she hath in all outward behaviours seem'd ever to abhor.

Benedick

Is't possible? Sits the wind in that corner?

Leonato

By my troth, my lord, I cannot tell what to think of it; but that she loves him with an enraged affection – it is past the infinite of thought.

Don Pedro

May be she doth but counterfeit.

105. ***came so near the life of passion*** imitated real passion so closely.

117. ***gull*** hoax.
118. ***knavery*** mischief.
119. ***reverence*** dignified speech and behaviour.

120. ***hold it up*** keep it going.

Claudio

Faith, like enough.

Leonato

O God, counterfeit! There was never counterfeit of passion came so near the life of passion as she discovers it:

Don Pedro

Why, what effects of passion shows she?

Claudio

Bait the hook well; this fish will bite.

Leonato

What effects, my lord? She will sit you – you heard my daughter tell you how.

Claudio

She did, indeed.

Don Pedro

How, how, I pray you? You amaze me; I would have thought her spirit had been invincible against all assaults of affection.

Leonato

I would have sworn it had, my lord; especially against Benedick.

Benedick

I should think this a gull, but that the white-bearded fellow speaks it; knavery cannot, sure, hide himself in such reverence.

Claudio

He hath ta'en th' infection; hold it up.

Don Pedro

Hath she made her affection known to Benedick?

Leonato

No; and swears she never will; that's her torment.

Claudio

'Tis true, indeed; so your daughter says. 'Shall I,' says she 'that have so oft encount'red him with scorn, write to him that I love him?'

Leonato

This says she now, when she is beginning to write to

128. ***smock*** undergarment.

131. ***jest*** joke.

133. ***sheet*** paper, and bed linen.

135. ***halfpence*** tiny fragments.

137. ***flout*** laugh at/scorn.

145. ***ecstasy*** mad passion.
145. ***overborne*** overcome.
147. ***outrage*** damage.

148–9. ***some other*** someone else.
149. ***discover*** reveal.

150. ***To what end?*** for what purpose?
150. ***sport*** joke.

152. ***alms*** good deed.

him; for she'll be up twenty times a night; and there will she sit in her smock till she have writ a sheet of paper. My daughter tells us all.

Claudio

Now you talk of a sheet of paper, I remember a pretty jest your daughter told us of.

Leonato

O, when she had writ it, and was reading it over, she found 'Benedick' and 'Beatrice' between the sheet!

Claudio

That.

Leonato

O, she tore the letter into a thousand halfpence; rail'd at herself that she should be so immodest to write to one that she knew would flout her. 'I measure him' says she 'by my own spirit; for I should flout him if he writ to me; yea, though I love him, I should.'

Claudio

Then down upon her knees she falls, weeps, sobs, beats her heart, tears her hair, prays, curses – 'O sweet Benedick! God give me patience!'

Leonato

She doth indeed; my daughter says so; and the ecstasy hath so much overborne her that my daughter is sometime afeard she will do a desperate outrage to herself. It is very true.

Don Pedro

It were good that Benedick knew of it by some other, if she will not discover it.

Claudio

To what end? He would make but a sport of it, and torment the poor lady worse.

Don Pedro

An he should, it were an alms to hang him. She's an excellent sweet lady, and, out of all suspicion, she is virtuous.

158. ***blood*** passion.

161. ***dotage*** affection.
162. ***daff'd*** put aside.
162–3. ***made her half myself*** married her.

169. ***bate*** give up.

171. ***tender*** an offer.

174. ***proper*** handsome.
175. ***happiness*** appearance.

178. ***valiant*** brave.

179. ***Hector*** a Trojan hero.

Claudio

And she is exceeding wise.

Don Pedro

In everything but in loving Benedick.

Leonato

O my lord, wisdom and blood combating in so tender a body, we have ten proofs to one that blood hath the victory. I am sorry for her, as I have just cause, being her uncle and her guardian.

Don Pedro

I would she had bestowed this dotage on me; I would have daff'd all other respects and made her half myself. I pray you, tell Benedick of it, and hear what 'a will say.

Leonato

Were it good, think you?

Claudio

Hero thinks surely she will die; for she says she will die if he love her not; and she will die ere she make her love known; and she will die if he woo her, rather than she will bate one breath of her accustomed crossness.

Don Pedro

She doth well; if she should make tender of her love, 'tis very possible he'll scorn it; for the man, as you know all, hath a contemptible spirit.

Claudio

He is a very proper man.

Don Pedro

He hath, indeed, a good outward happiness.

Claudio

Before God, and in my mind, very wise!

Don Pedro

He doth, indeed, show some sparks that are like wit.

Leonato

And I take him to be valiant.

Don Pedro

As Hector, I assure you; and in the managing of

183. ***'a must*** he must.

187. ***howsoever*** even though.

191. ***counsel*** reflection.

205–6. ***dumb show*** meaningful gestures without speech.

quarrels you may say he is wise, for either he avoids them with great discretion, or undertakes them with a most Christian-like fear.

Leonato

If he do fear God, 'a must necessarily keep peace; if he break the peace, he ought to enter into a quarrel with fear and trembling.

Don Pedro

And so will he do; for the man doth fear God, howsoever it seems not in him by some large jests he will make. Well, I am sorry for your niece. Shall we go seek Benedick, and tell him of her love?

Claudio

Never tell him, my lord; let her wear it out with good counsel.

Leonato

Nay, that's impossible; she may wear her heart out first.

Don Pedro

Well, we will hear further of it by your daughter; let it cool the while. I love Benedick well; and I could wish he would modestly examine himself, to see how much he is unworthy so good a lady.

Leonato

My lord, will you walk? Dinner is ready.

Claudio

If he do not dote on her upon this, I will never trust my expectation.

Don Pedro

Let there be the same net spread for her; and that must your daughter and her gentlewomen carry. The sport will be when they hold one an opinion of another's dotage, and no such matter; that's the scene that I would see, which will be merely a dumb show. Let us send her to call him in to dinner.

[Exeunt DON PEDRO, CLAUDIO, *and* LEONATO.*]*

208. ***sadly*** seriously.

211. ***requited*** returned.
211. ***censur'd*** judged.

216. ***detractions*** faults.

219. ***reprove*** deny.

222–3. ***remnants of wit broken on me jokes*** made at my expense.

225. ***meat*** food.

227. ***awe*** scare.
229. ***peopled*** populated.

231. ***marks*** signs.

Benedick

[Coming forward] This can be no trick: the conference was sadly borne; they have the truth of this from Hero; they seem to pity the lady; it seems her affections have their full bent. Love me! Why, it must be requited. I hear how I am censur'd: they say I will bear myself proudly if I perceive the love come from her; they say, too, that she will rather die than give any sign of affection. I did never think to marry. I must not seem proud; happy are they that hear their detractions and can put them to mending. They say the lady is fair; 'tis a truth, I can bear them witness; and virtuous; 'tis so, I cannot reprove it; and wise, but for loving me. By my troth, it is no addition to her wit; nor no great argument of her folly, for I will be horribly in love with her. I may chance have some odd quirks and remnants of wit broken on me because I have railed so long against marriage; but doth not the appetite alter? A man loves the meat in his youth that he cannot endure in his age. Shall quips, and sentences, and these paper bullets of the brain, awe a man from the career of his humour? No; the world must be peopled. When I said I would die a bachelor, I did not think I should live till I were married. Here comes Beatrice. By this day, she's a fair lady; I do spy some marks of love in her.

[Enter BEATRICE.*]*

Beatrice

Against my will I am sent to bid you come in to dinner.

Benedick

Fair Beatrice, I thank you for your pains.

Beatrice

I took no more pains for those thanks than you take pains to thank me; if it had been painful, I would not have come.

241. ***daw*** jackdaw (a bird rather like a magpie).
242. ***stomach*** appetite.

249. ***Jew*** here used to mean an 'object of abuse', reflecting contemporary ideas about anti-Christian (and therefore immoral) races.

Benedick

You take pleasure, then, in the message?

Beatrice

Yea, just so much as you may take upon a knife's point, and choke a daw withal. You have no stomach, signior; fare you well.

[Exit.]

Benedick

Ha! 'Against my will I am sent to bid you come in to dinner' – there's a double meaning in that. 'I took no more pains for those thanks than you took pains to thank me' – that's as much as to say 'Any pains that I take for you is as easy as thanks'. If I do not take pity of her, I am a villain; if I do not love her, I am a Jew. I will go get her picture.

[Exit.]

ACT III SCENE I

This scene is, of course, the twin to Act 2 Scene 3 in which Benedick is fooled by Don Pedro and company. The same techniques are used here; while the victim 'hides', the plotters heap praise on the other person. In this case, Benedick is described as 'so rare a gentleman' and with an 'excellent good name'. Conversely, the victim is heavily critiicised; Hero says of Beatrice – 'She cannot love, Nor take no shape nor project of affection, She is so self-endeared . . .' For both Beatrice and Benedick these scenes are chastening experiences, holding a sort of mirror up to who they are, or have been, but offering the chance for redemption and transformation.

3. ***proposing*** talking.

5. ***discourse*** conversation.

7. ***pleached*** covered with twisted branches.
7. ***bower*** leafy garden shelter.
9. ***favourites*** favoured members of the court.

12. ***propose*** conversation.
12. ***office*** task.

14. ***presently*** at once.

16. ***trace*** walk.

ACT THREE

Scene I

Leonato's orchard

[Enter HERO, MARGARET, *and* URSULA.*]*

Hero

Good Margaret, run thee to the parlour;
There shall thou find my cousin Beatrice
Proposing with the Prince and Claudio.
Whisper her ear, and tell her I and Ursula
Walk in the orchard, and our whole discourse
Is all of her; say that thou overheard'st us;
And bid her steal into the pleached bower,
Where honeysuckles, ripened by the sun,
Forbid the sun to enter – like favourites,
Made proud by princes, that advance their pride
Against that power that bred it. There will she hide her
To listen our propose. This is thy office;
Bear thee well in it, and leave us alone.

Margaret

I'll make her come, I warrant you, presently.

[Exit.]

Hero

Now, Ursula, when Beatrice doth come,
As we do trace this alley up and down,
Our talk must only be of Benedick.
When I do name him, let it be thy part
To praise him more than ever man did merit;
My talk to thee must be how Benedick
Is sick in love with Beatrice. Of this matter
Is little Cupid's crafty arrow made,
That only wounds by hearsay. Now begin;

24. ***lapwing*** a bird which flies near to the ground.

30. ***couched*** hidden.
30. ***woodbine*** honeysuckle.
30. ***coverture*** shelter.

36. ***haggards*** untamed hawk.

38. ***trothed*** engaged.

42. ***wrestle with affection*** fight against his feelings.

49. ***fram'd*** formed.
50. ***stuff*** material.

[Enter BEATRICE, *behind.]*

For look where Beatrice, like a lapwing, runs
Close by the ground, to hear our conference.

Ursula

The pleasant'st angling is to see the fish
Cut with her golden oars the silver stream,
And greedily devour the treacherous bait.
So angle we for Beatrice; who even now
Is couched in the woodbine coverture.
Fear you not my part of the dialogue.

Hero

Then go we near her, that her ear lose nothing
Of the false sweet bait that we lay for it.

[They advance to the bower.]

No, truly, Ursula, she is too disdainful;
I know her spirits are as coy and wild
As haggards of the rock.

Ursula

But are you sure
That Benedick loves Beatrice so entirely?

Hero

So says the Prince and my new-trothed lord.

Ursula

And did they bid you tell her of it, madam?

Hero

They did entreat me to acquaint her of it;
But I persuaded them, if they lov'd Benedick,
To wish him wrestle with affection,
And never to let Beatrice know of it.

Ursula

Why did you so? Doth not the gentleman
Deserve as full as fortunate a bed
As ever Beatrice shall couch upon?

Hero

O god of love! I know he doth deserve
As much as may be yielded to a man;

52. ***Misprising*** undervaluing.

55. ***project*** idea.
56. ***self-endeared*** fond of herself.

58. ***sport*** mockery.

61. ***spell him backward*** view the virtues of a man as faults.

63. ***Nature, drawing of an antic, Made a foul blot*** While in the process of drawing a cartoon-like clown made a real mess.
64. ***lance ill-headed*** spear with a poorly-crafted tip.
65. ***agate*** very vilely cut poorly-crafted gem.
66. ***vane*** weathervane.

70. ***simpleness*** plain honesty.

71. ***carping*** complaining.

72. ***from all fashions*** out of step with the rest of the world.

75. ***into air*** out of existence.

But nature never fram'd a woman's heart
Of prouder stuff than that of Beatrice.
Disdain and scorn ride sparkling in her eyes,
Misprising what they look on; and her wit
Values itself so highly that to her
All matter else seems weak. She cannot love,
Nor take no shape nor project of affection,
She is so self-endeared.

Ursula

Sure, I think so;
And therefore, certainly, it were not good
She knew his love, lest she'll make sport at it.

Hero

Why, you speak truth. I never yet saw man,
How wise, how noble, young, how rarely featur'd,
But she would spell him backward. If fair-fac'd,
She would swear the gentleman should be her sister;
If black, why. Nature, drawing of an antic,
Made a foul blot; if tall, a lance ill-headed;
If low, an agate very vilely cut;
If speaking, why, a vane blown with all winds;
If silent, why, a block moved with none.
So turns she every man the wrong side out,
And never gives to truth and virtue that
Which simpleness and merit purchaseth.

Ursula

Sure, sure, such carping is not commendable.

Hero

No; not to be so odd and from all fashions,
As Beatrice is, cannot be commendable;
But who dare tell her so? If I should speak,
She would mock me into air; O, she would laugh me
Out of myself, press me to death with wit!
Therefore let Benedick, like cover'd fire,
Consume away in sighs, waste inwardly.
It were a better death than die with mocks,
Which is as bad as die with tickling.

83. ***counsel*** advise.
84. ***honest slanders*** insults that will not harm Beatrice's reputation.

90. ***priz'd*** reputed.

95. ***my fancy*** my mind/imagination.
96. ***argument*** intelligent debate.

101. ***every day – tomorrow*** from tomorrow onwards.

103. ***to furnish me*** provide for me to wear.

104. ***lim'd*** trapped.

105. ***by haps*** by chance.

Ursula
Yet tell her of it; hear what she will say.

Hero
No; rather I will go to Benedick
And counsel him to fight against his passion;
And, truly, I'll devise some honest slanders
To stain my cousin with. One doth not know
How much an ill word may empoison liking.

Ursula
O, do not do your cousin such a wrong!
She cannot be so much without true judgment –
Having so swift and excellent a wit
As she is priz'd to have – as to refuse
So rare a gentleman as Signior Benedick.

Hero
He is the only man of Italy,
Always excepted my dear Claudio.

Ursula
I pray you be not angry with me, madam,
Speaking my fancy: Signior Benedick,
For shape, for bearing, argument, and valour,
Goes foremost in report through Italy.

Hero
Indeed, he hath an excellent good name.

Ursula
His excellence did earn it ere he had it.
When are you married, madam?

Hero
Why, every day – to-morrow. Come, go in;
I'll show thee some attires, and have thy counsel
Which is the best to furnish me to-morrow.

Ursula
She's lim'd, I warrant you; we have caught her, madam.

Hero
If it prove so, then loving goes by haps:
Some Cupid kills with arrows, some with traps.

[*Exeunt* HERO *and* URSULA.]

114. ***band*** marriage bond.

116. ***reportingly*** just by reputation.

Beatrice

[Coming forward] What fire is in mine ears? Can this be true?
Stand I condemn'd for pride and scorn so much?
Contempt, farewell! and maiden pride, adieu!
No glory lives behind the back of such.
And, Benedick, love on; I will requite thee,
Taming my wild heart to thy loving hand;
If thou dost love, my kindness shall incite thee
To bind our loves up in a holy band;
For others say thou dost deserve, and I
Believe it better than reportingly.

[Exit.]

SCENE II

This scene signals a real turning point as the action switches from the light-hearted comedy surrounding Benedick's lovesick behaviour, to the nasty and vindictive trickery of Don John. As Don Pedro says at the end: 'O day untowardly turned' (What a turn for the worse!) Although the audience know Hero is innocent, Claudio and Don Pedro do not – but the idea of shaming her in front of everyone is a deeply-unpleasant idea in itself. What is also interesting is how little they question or mistrust Don John. This may seem realistic given Claudio's youth, but is more questionable given Don Pedro's stature and nobility.

1. ***consummate*** completed.
3. ***bring*** escort.
3. ***vouchsafe*** permit.
5. ***soil*** stain.
7. ***bold with*** forward in asking.

15. *Gallants* gentlemen.

Scene II

Leonato's house.

[Enter DON PEDRO, CLAUDIO, BENEDICK, *and* LEONATO.*]*

Don Pedro

I do but stay till your marriage be consummate, and then go I toward Arragon.

Claudio

I'll bring you thither, my lord, if you'll vouchsafe me.

Don Pedro

Nay, that would be as great a soil in the new gloss of your marriage as to show a child his new coat, and forbid him to wear it. I will only be bold with Benedick for his company; for, from the crown of his head to the sole of his foot, he is all mirth; he hath twice or thrice cut Cupid's bow-string, and the little hangman dare not shoot at him; he hath a heart as sound as a bell, and his tongue is the clapper; for what his heart thinks, his tongue speaks.

Benedick

Gallants, I am not as I have been.

Leonato

So say I; methinks you are sadder.

Claudio

I hope he be in love.

Don Pedro

Hang him, truant! There's no true drop of blood in him to be truly touch'd with love; if he be sad, he wants money.

Benedick

I have the toothache.

Don Pedro

Draw it.

26. ***humour or a worm*** both were thought to cause toothache by collecting in decayed teeth.
27. ***grief*** misery, woe.

30. ***fancy*** love, or affectation.

34. ***slops*** large, loose breeches (type of trousers).

40. ***bode*** foretell.

43–4. ***old ornament of his cheek hath already stuff'd tennis balls*** the beard he used to have has been shaved off.

47. ***civet*** perfume.

Benedick
Hang it!

Claudio
You must hang it first and draw it afterwards.

Don Pedro
What! sigh for the toothache?

Leonato
Where is but a humour or a worm.

Benedick
Well, every one can master a grief but he that has it.

Claudio
Yet, say I, he is in love.

Don Pedro
There is no appearance of fancy in him, unless it be a fancy that he hath to strange disguises; as to be a Dutchman today, a Frenchman to-morrow; or in the shape of two countries at once, as a German from the waist downward, all slops, and a Spaniard from the hip upward, no doublet. Unless he have a fancy to this foolery, as it appears he hath, he is no fool for fancy, as you would have it appear he is.

Claudio
If he be not in love with some woman, there is no believing old signs: 'a brushes his hat o' mornings; what should that bode?

Don Pedro
Hath any man seen him at the barber's?

Claudio
No, but the barber's man hath been seen with him; and the old ornament of his cheek hath already stuff'd tennis-balls.

Leonato
Indeed, he looks younger than he did, by the loss of a beard.

Don Pedro
Nay, 'a rubs himself with civet. Can you smell him out by that?

51. ***wash his face*** use cosmetics.

52. ***paint himself*** use make-up.

55. ***lute*** stringed instrument, a little like a guitar, that often accompanied love songs.
55. ***stops*** frets on the lute.

61. ***ill conditions*** bad habits.

64. ***charm*** cure.

66–7. ***hobby-horses*** fools, buffoons.

Claudio
That's as much as to say the sweet youth's in love.

Don Pedro
The greatest note of it is his melancholy

Claudio
And when was he wont to wash his face?

Don Pedro
Yea, or to paint himself? For the which I hear what they say of him.

Claudio
Nay, but his jesting spirit, which is now crept into a lute-string, and now govern'd by stops.

Don Pedro
Indeed, that tells a heavy tale for him; conclude, conclude, he is in love.

Claudio
Nay, but I know who loves him.

Don Pedro
That would I know too; I warrant, one that knows him not.

Claudio
Yes, and his ill conditions; and, in despite of all, dies for him.

Don Pedro
She shall be buried with her face upwards.

Benedick
Yet is this no charm for the toothache. Old signior, walk aside with me; I have studied eight or nine wise words to speak to you, which these hobby-horses must not hear.

[*Exeunt* BENEDICK *and* LEONATO.]

Don Pedro
For my life, to break with him about Beatrice.

Claudio
'Tis even so. Hero and Margaret have by this played their parts with Beatrice; and then the two bears will not bite one another when they meet.

73. ***Good den*** good evening.

83. ***impediment*** obstruction.

85. ***aim better at me*** form a better opinion of me.
86. ***manifest*** show.
87. ***holp to effect*** helped to bring about.
88. ***suit*** effort.
89. ***ill bestowed*** misused.

93. ***disloyal*** unfaithful.

[Enter DON JOHN.*]*

Don John
My lord and brother. God save you!

Don Pedro
Good den, brother.

Don John
If your leisure serv'd, I would speak with you.

Don Pedro
In private?

Don John
If it please you; yet Count Claudio may hear, for what I would speak of concerns him.

Don Pedro
What's the matter?

Don John
[To CLAUDIO*]* Means your lordship to be married tomorrow?

Don Pedro
You know he does.

Don John
I know not that, when he knows what I know.

Claudio
If there be any impediment, I pray you discover it.

Don John
You may think I love you not; let that appear hereafter, and aim better at me by that I now will manifest. For my brother, I think he holds you well, and in dearness of heart hath holp to effect your ensuing marriage – surely suit ill spent, and labour ill bestowed.

Don Pedro
Why, what's the matter?

Don John
I came hither to tell you; and, circumstances short'ned, for she has been too long a talking of, the lady is disloyal.

98. ***paint out*** fully depict, describe.

101. ***warrant*** evidence.

118. ***bear it coldly*** control your anger.
119. ***issue*** outcome.

Claudio
Who? Hero?

Don John
Even she – Leonato's Hero, your Hero, every man's Hero.

Claudio
Disloyal?

Don John
The word is too good to paint out her wickedness; I could say she were worse; think you of a worse title, and I will fit her to it. Wonder not till further warrant; go but with me to-night, you shall see her chamber window ent'red, even the night before her wedding-day. If you love her then, to-morrow wed her; but it would better fit your honour to change your mind.

Claudio
May this be so?

Don Pedro
I will not think it.

Don John
If you dare not trust that you see, confess not that you know. If you will follow me, I will show you enough; and when you have seen more, and heard more, proceed accordingly.

Claudio
If I see anything to-night why I should not marry her, to-morrow in the congregation where I should wed, there will I shame her.

Don Pedro
And, as I wooed for thee to obtain her, I will join with thee to disgrace her.

Don John
I will disparage her no farther till you are my witnesses; bear it coldly but till midnight, and let the issue show itself.

Don Pedro
O day untowardly turned!

Claudio

O mischief strangely thwarting!

Don John

O plague right well prevented! So will you say when you have seen the sequel.

[Exeunt.]

SCENE III

This scene – almost halfway through the play – introduces the new characters of Dogberry, Verges and the Watch – all comic characters, but presented as decent and honest. Their lack of intelligence (for example, mixing up of words by mistake: Dogberry calls one of the Watch officers 'senseless' when he means 'sensible') contrasts with the elaborate wit of Don Pedro, Benedick and company. The scene is also important dramatically because it means the audience knows that Don John's treachery is likely to be revealed – at some point.

7. ***charge*** duties.
8. ***desartless*** a malapropism ('desert-less') for 'deserving' – thus meaning the exact opposite!
9. ***constable*** leader of the 'Watch'.

13. ***well-favoured*** good-looking.

21. ***senseless*** a malapropism for 'sensible'.

Scene III

A street.

[Enter DOGBERRY *and his compartner* VERGES, *with the* WATCH.*]*

Dogberry

Are you good men and true?

Verges

Yea, or else it were pity but they should suffer salvation, body and soul.

Dogberry

Nay, that were a punishment too good for them, if they should have any allegiance in them, being chosen for the Prince's watch.

Verges

Well, give them their charge, neighbour Dogberry.

Dogberry

First, who think you the most desartless man to be constable?

1 Watch

Hugh Oatcake, sir, or George Seacoal; for they can write and read.

Dogberry

Come hither, neighbour Seacoal. God hath bless'd you with a good name. To be a well-favoured man is the gift of fortune; but to write and read comes by nature.

2 Watch

Both which. Master Constable –

Dogberry

You have; I knew it would be your answer. Well, for your favour, sir, why, give God thanks, and make no boast of it; and for your writing and reading, let that appear when there is no need of such vanity. You are thought here to be the most senseless and fit man for the constable of the watch; therefore bear you the

24. ***comprehend*** a malapropism for 'apprehend'.
24. ***vagrom*** tramp, drifter (like 'vagrant').
26. ***How if 'a will not stand?*** what if he won't stop?

30. ***bidden*** told to.

35. ***tolerable*** Dogberry means the opposite 'intolerable' (i.e unbearable).

37. ***belongs to a watch*** in keeping with how a watchman should behave.

38. ***ancient*** experienced.

40. ***bills*** weapons.

49. ***true*** honest.

lantern. This is your charge: you shall comprehend all vagrom men; you are to bid any man stand, in the Prince's name.

2 Watch

How if 'a will not stand?

Dogberry

Why, then, take no note of him, but let him go; and presently call the rest of the watch together, and thank God you are rid of a knave.

Verges

If he will not stand when he is bidden, he is none of the Prince's subjects.

Dogberry

True, and they are to meddle with none but the Prince's subjects. You shall also make no noise in the streets; for for the watch to babble and to talk is most tolerable and not to be endured.

2 Watch

We will rather sleep than talk; we know what belongs to a watch.

Dogberry

Why, you speak like an ancient and most quiet watchman, for I cannot see how sleeping should offend; only, have a care that your bills be not stol'n. Well, you are to call at all the ale-houses, and bid those that are drunk get them to bed.

2 Watch

How if they will not?

Dogberry

Why, then, let them alone till they are sober; if they make you not then the better answer, you may say they are not the men you took them for.

2 Watch

Well, sir.

Dogberry

If you meet a thief, you may suspect him, by virtue of your office, to be no true man; and, for such kind of men, the less you meddle or make with them, why,

54–5. ***they that touch pitch will be defil'd*** a saying meaning 'those that touch tar will be made filthy'.

71. ***present*** represent.

75. ***statutes*** law.

the more is for your honesty.

2 Watch

If we know him to be a thief, shall we not lay hands on him?

Dogberry

Truly, by your office you may, but I think they that touch pitch will be defil'd; the most peaceable way for you, if you do take a thief, is to let him show himself what he is, and steal out of your company.

Verges

You have been always called a merciful man, partner.

Dogberry

Truly, I would not hang a dog by my will, much more a man who hath any honesty in him.

Verges

If you hear a child cry in the night, you must call to the nurse and bid her still it.

2 Watch

How if the nurse be asleep and will not hear us?

Dogberry

Why, then, depart in peace, and let the child wake her with crying; for the ewe that will not hear her lamb when it baes will never answer a calf when he bleats.

Verges

'Tis very true.

Dogberry

This is the end of the charge: you, constable, are to present the Prince's own person; if you meet the Prince in the night, you may stay him.

Verges

Nay, by'r lady, that I think 'a cannot.

Dogberry

Five shillings to one on't, with any man that knows the statutes, he may stay him; marry, not without the Prince be willing; for, indeed, the watch ought to offend no man, and it is an offence to stay a man against his will.

81. ***matter of weight chances*** anything important happens.
81–2. ***keep your fellows' counsels and your own*** be discreet (don't speak to other people about this).

88. ***coil*** racket.
89. ***vigitant*** Dogberry means 'vigilant' ('watchful').

94. ***my elbow itch'd*** believed to be an omen of bad company.
95. ***scab*** rogue, traitor.

98. ***penthouse*** shed or sloping porch.

Verges
By'r lady, I think it be so.

Dogberry
Ha, ah, ha! Well, masters, good night; an there be any matter of weight chances, call up me; keep your fellows' counsels and your own, and good night. Come, neighbour.

2 Watch
Well, masters, we hear our charge; let us go sit here upon the church bench till two, and then all to bed.

Dogberry
One word more, honest neighbours: I pray you watch about Signior Leonato's door; for the wedding being there to-morrow, there is a great coil to-night. Adieu; be vigitant, I beseech you.

[*Exeunt* DOGBERRY *and* VERGES.]

[*Enter* BORACHIO *and* CONRADE.]

Borachio
What, Conrade!

2 Watch
[*Aside*] Peace, stir not.

Borachio
Conrade, I say!

Conrade
Here, man, I am at thy elbow.

Borachio
Mass, and my elbow itch'd; I thought there would a scab follow.

Conrade
Will owe thee an answer for that; and now forward with thy tale.

Borachio
Stand thee close then under this penthouse, for it drizzles rain; and I will, like a true drunkard, utter all to thee.

101. ***stand close*** stay quiet.

107. ***make*** ask.

110. ***unconfirm'd*** inexperienced.

112. ***nothing to a man*** different from the man himself.

2 Watch
[Aside] Some treason, masters; yet stand close.

Borachio
Therefore know I have earned of Don John a thousand ducats.

Conrade
Is it possible that any villainy should be so dear?

Borachio
Thou shouldst rather ask if it were possible any villainy should be so rich; for when rich villains have need of poor ones, poor ones may make what price they will.

Conrade
I wonder at it.

Borachio
That shows thou art unconfirm'd. Thou knowest that the fashion of a doublet, or a hat, or a cloak, is nothing to a man.

Conrade
Yes, it is apparel.

Borachio
I mean the fashion.

Conrade
Yes, the fashion is the fashion.

Borachio
Tush! I may as well say the fool's the fool. But seest thou not what a deformed thief this fashion is?

2 Watch
[Aside] I know that Deformed; 'a has been a vile thief this seven year; 'a goes up and down like a gentleman; I remember his name.

Borachio
Didst thou not hear somebody?

Conrade
No; 'twas the vane on the house.

Borachio
Seest thou not, I say, what a deformed thief this fashion is, how giddily 'a turns about all the hot bloods between

126. ***Pharaoh's soldiers*** in the Bible, Pharoah and his soldiers drowned as they chased the escaping Israelites.
127. ***reechy*** grimy.
127–8. ***god Bel's priests*** in the Bible, priests who were killed when Daniel accused them of forcing the people to accept a false god.
129. ***smirch'd*** dirty.
130. ***codpiece*** pouch worn at the front of men's trousers.

133–4. ***shifted out*** changed out (as with a shirt).

141. ***possessed*** influenced.

150. ***he was appointed*** he had arranged.

152–3. ***o'er night*** the previous night.

154. ***charge*** order.

156. ***recover'd*** a malapropism for 'discovered'.
156. ***lechery*** a malapropism for 'treachery' (lechery – distasteful sexual behaviour).
157. ***commonwealth*** country or state.

fourteen and five and thirty, sometimes fashioning them like Pharaoh's soldiers in the reechy painting, sometime like god Bel's priests in the old church-window, sometime like the shaven Hercules in the smirch'd worm-eaten tapestry, where his codpiece seems as massy as his club?

Conrade

All this I see; and I see that the fashion wears out more apparel than the man. But art not thou thyself giddy with the fashion too, that thou hast shifted out of thy tale into telling me of the fashion?

Borachio

Not so neither; but know that I have to-night wooed Margaret, the Lady Hero's gentlewoman, by the name of Hero; she leans me out at her mistress' chamber-window, bids me a thousand times good night – I tell this tale vilely. I should first tell thee how the Prince, Claudio, and my master, planted and placed and possessed by my master Don John, saw afar off in the orchard this amiable encounter.

Conrade

And thought they Margaret was Hero?

Borachio

Two of them did, the Prince and Claudio; but the devil my master knew she was Margaret; and partly by his oaths, which first possess'd them, partly by the dark night, which did deceive them, but chiefly by my villainy, which did confirm any slander that Don John had made, away went Claudio enrag'd; swore he would meet her, as he was appointed, next morning at the temple, and there, before the whole congregation, shame her with what he saw o'er night, and send her home again without a husband.

2 Watch

We charge you in the Prince's name, stand.

1 Watch

Call up the right Master Constable; we have here recover'd the most dangerous piece of lechery that ever was known in the commonwealth.

2 Watch

And one Deformed is one of them; I know him, 'a wears a lock.

Conrade

Masters, masters!

2 Watch

You'll be made bring Deformed forth, I warrant you.

Conrade

Masters –

1 Watch

Never speak, we charge you; let us obey you to go with us.

Borachio

We are like to prove a goodly commodity, being taken up of these men's bills.

Conrade

A commodity in question, I warrant you. Come, we'll obey you.

[Exeunt.]

SCENE IV

This short scene is a busy, active interlude before the grander drama of what is to come. We can imagine Hero nervously getting ready for her 'big day', trying on outfits, with maidservants coming rushing in and out of the room. But the scene also reveals how much Beatrice has changed – she is now depicted as the fool who is in love (and doesn't seem to know it) and is even outwitted (in jokes) by Margaret, her cousin's gentlewoman.

6. ***rabato*** a stiff collar or ruff, particularly popular in Shakespeare's day.

11. ***tire*** head-dress (similar to 'attire').

16. ***exceeds*** excels.

19. ***down sleeves*** long sleeves to the wrist.
19. ***side sleeves*** sleeves open from the shoulder.

Scene IV

Hero's apartment.

[Enter HERO, MARGARET, *and* URSULA.*]*

Hero

Good Ursula, wake my cousin Beatrice, and desire her to rise.

Ursula

I will, lady.

Hero

And bid her come hither.

Ursula

Well.

[Exit URSULA.*]*

Margaret

Troth, I think your other rabato were better.

Hero

No, pray thee, good Meg, I'll wear this.

Margaret

By my troth's not so good; and I warrant your cousin will say so.

Hero

My cousin's a fool, and thou art another; I'll wear none but this.

Margaret

I like the new tire within excellently, if the hair were a thought browner; and your gown's a most rare fashion, i' faith. I saw the Duchess of Milan's gown that they praise so.

Hero

O, that exceeds, they say.

Margaret

By my troth's but a night-gown in respect of yours – cloth o' gold, and cuts, and lac'd with silver, set with pearls, down sleeves, side sleeves, and skirts,

21. ***quaint*** dainty.

26. ***Fie*** shame.

31. ***wrest*** twist (like 'wrestle').

34. ***light*** immoral.
35. ***else*** otherwise.

38. ***how now*** what's the matter.

40. ***Clap's into*** let us break into.
40. ***light o' love*** a popular dance, but could also refer to a loose woman.
40–1. ***without a burden lightly***, and without a male vocal accompaniment.
42. ***with your heels*** unchastely.
44. ***barns*** a pun on the word 'bairns', meaning children.

round underborne with a bluish tinsel; but for a fine, quaint, graceful, and excellent fashion, yours is worth ten on't.

Hero

God give me joy to wear it, for my heart is exceeding heavy.

Margaret

'Twill be heavier soon, by the weight of a man.

Hero

Fie upon thee! art not ashamed?

Margaret

Of what, lady, of speaking honourably? Is not marriage honourable in a beggar? Is not your lord honourable without marriage? I think you would have me say 'saving your reverence, a husband'; an bad thinking do not wrest true speaking I'll offend nobody. Is there any harm in 'the heavier for a husband'? None, I think, an it be the right husband and the right wife; otherwise 'tis light, and not heavy. Ask my Lady Beatrice else; here she comes.

[*Enter* BEATRICE.]

Hero

Good morrow, coz.

Beatrice

Good morrow, sweet Hero.

Hero

Why, how now! do you speak in the sick tune?

Beatrice

I am out of all other tune, methinks.

Margaret

Clap's into 'Light o' love'; that goes without a burden. Do you sing it, and I'll dance it.

Beatrice

Ye light o' love with your heels! Then if your husband have stables enough, you'll see he shall lack no barnes.

48. ***Heigh-ho*** a sigh, also used to call hawks and horses.

50. ***H*** pronounced 'ache' or 'aitch'.

51. ***turned Turk*** changed your views.
52. ***star*** Pole Star (i.e. a fixed point).

53. ***trow*** I wonder.

58. ***am stuff'd*** have a head cold (could also mean pregnant).

61. ***apprehension*** quick wit.

66. ***Carduus benedictus*** Holy Thistle, considered a cure for many illnesses.
68. ***qualm*** sudden illness.

Margaret
O illegitimate construction! I scorn that with my heels.

Beatrice
'Tis almost five o'clock, cousin; 'tis time you were ready. By my troth, I am exceeding ill. Heigh-ho!

Margaret
For a hawk, a horse, or a husband?

Beatrice
For the letter that begins them all – H.

Margaret
Well, an you be not turn'd Turk, there's no more sailing by the star.

Beatrice
What means the fool, trow?

Margaret
Nothing I; but God send every one their heart's desire!

Hero
These gloves the Count sent me; they are an excellent perfume.

Beatrice
I am stuff'd, cousin, I cannot smell.

Margaret
A maid and stuff'd! There's goodly catching of cold.

Beatrice
O, God help me! God help me! How long have you profess'd apprehension?

Margaret
Ever since you left it. Doth not my wit become me rarely?

Beatrice
It is not seen enough; you should wear it in your cap. By my troth, I am sick.

Margaret
Get you some of this distill'd Carduus Benedictus, and lay it to your heart; it is the only thing for a qualm.

70. ***moral*** hidden meaning, or message.

75. ***list*** wish.

83. ***eats his meat without grudging*** accepts his fate (i.e. to get married) without complaint.

87. ***false gallop*** an unnatural burst of speed, i.e. truth.

Hero
There thou prick'st her with a thistle.

Beatrice
Benedictus! why Benedictus? You have some moral in this 'Benedictus'.

Margaret
Moral? No, by my troth, I have no moral meaning; I meant plain holy-thistle. You may think, perchance, that I think you are in love. Nay, by'r lady, I am not such a fool to think what I list; nor I list not to think what I can; nor, indeed, I cannot think, if I would think my heart out of thinking, that you are in love, or that you will be in love, or that you can be in love. Yet Benedick was such another, and now is he become a man; he swore he would never marry, and yet now, in despite of his heart, he eats his meat without grudging. And how you may be converted I know not; but methinks you look with your eyes as other women do.

Beatrice
What pace is this that thy tongue keeps?

Margaret
Not a false gallop.

[Re-enter URSULA.*]*

Ursula
Madam, withdraw; the Prince, the Count, Signior Benedick, Don John, and all the gallants of the town, are come to fetch you to church.

Hero
Help to dress me, good coz, good Meg, good Ursula.

[Exeunt.]

SCENE V

The last scene of this Act creates huge dramatic tension as Dogberry and Verges attempt to tell Leonato about the villains they have 'comprehended' (they mean 'apprehended'). Their confusing explanation is seen by Leonato as a trivial matter which is interfering with his preparations for his daughter's wedding, and he orders them to carry out the interrogation themselves, thus missing a chance to avoid the humiliation that awaits him and Hero.

3. ***nearly*** closely.

9. ***Goodman*** title of a man below the rank of gentleman.

15. ***palabras*** a few words.

Scene V

Leonato's house.

[Enter LEONATO, *with* DOGBERRY *and* VERGES.*]*

Leonato

What would you with me, honest neighbour?

Dogberry

Marry, sir, I would have some confidence with you that decerns you nearly.

Leonato

Brief, I pray you; for you see it is a busy time with me.

Dogberry

Marry, this it is, sir

Verges

Yes, in truth it is, sir.

Leonato

What is it, my good friends?

Dogberry

Goodman Verges, sir, speaks a little off the matter – an old man, sir, and his wits are not so blunt as. God help, I would desire they were; but, in faith, honest as the skin between his brows.

Verges

Yes, I thank God I am as honest as any man living that is an old man and no honester than I.

Dogberry

Comparisons are odorous; palabras, neighbour Verges.

Leonato

Neighbours, you are tedious.

Dogberry

It pleases your worship to say so, but we are the poor Duke's officers; but, truly, for mine own part, if I were as tedious as a king, I could find in my heart to bestow it all of your worship.

24. ***exclamation*** Dogberry means 'acclamation' (praise).

28. ***fain know*** be glad to know.

30. ***ha' ta'en*** have arrested.
30–31. ***arrant knaves*** completely dishonest men.

34. ***world*** wonder.

Leonato
All thy tediousness on me, ah?

Dogberry
Yea, an 'twere a thousand pound more than 'tis; for I hear as good exclamation on your worship as of any man in the city; and though I be but a poor man, I am glad to hear it.

Verges
And so am I.

Leonato
I would fain know what you have to say.

Verges
Marry, sir, our watch to-night, excepting your worship's presence, ha' ta'en a couple of as arrant knaves as any in Messina.

Dogberry
A good old man, sir, he will be talking; as they say 'When the age is in the wit is out'. God help us, it is a world to see! Well said, i' faith, neighbour Verges; well. God's a good man; an two men ride of a horse, one must ride behind. An honest soul, i' faith, sir, by my troth he is, as ever broke bread; but God is to be worshipp'd; all men are not alike; alas, good neighbour!

Leonato
Indeed, neighbour, he comes too short of you.

Dogberry
Gifts that God gives.

Leonato
I must leave you.

Dogberry
One word, sir: our watch, sir, have indeed comprehended two aspicious persons, and we would have them this morning examined before your worship;

Leonato
Take their examination yourself, and bring it me; I am now in great haste, as it may appear unto you.

59. ***non-come*** bewilderment, confusion.

Dogberry

It shall be suffigance.

Leonato

Drink some wine ere you go; fare you well.

[Enter a MESSENGER.*]*

Messenger

My lord, they stay for you to give your daughter to her husband.

Leonato

I'll wait upon them; I am ready.

[Exeunt LEONATO *and* MESSENGER.*]*

Dogberry

Go, good partner, go, get you to Francis Seacoal; bid him bring his pen and inkhorn to the gaol; we are now to examination these men

Verges

And we must do it wisely. Dogberry We will spare for no wit, I warrant you; here's that shall drive some of them to a non-come; only get the learned writer to set down our excommunication, and meet me at the gaol.

[Exeunt.]

ACT IV SCENE 1

Because we know Hero is innocent, this scene – at the heart of a comedy – is all the more powerful. Claudio's words – calling her a 'rotten orange', and her own father's – saying she has 'foul-tainted flesh', are shocking and unpleasant, and it's impossible not to feel sympathy for Hero. Claudio and Don Pedro, even though they have been deceived, come out of the scene badly; the speed with which Claudio, in particular, rushes to condemn Hero shows that he is still young – and lacks wisdom. In contrast, Beatrice and the Friar both realise something isn't right – and even Benedick sees that Don John may be behind it all (he says; 'the practice of it lives in John . . . Whose spirits toil in frame of villainies . . .')

1. ***plain*** most basic.
2. ***particular*** specific.

9. ***inward impediment*** secret objection.
10. ***charge*** order.

ACT FOUR

Scene I

A church.

[Enter DON PEDRO, DON JOHN, LEONATO, FRIAR FRANCIS, CLAUDIO, BENEDICK, HERO, BEATRICE, *and Attendants.]*

Leonato

Come, Friar Francis, be brief; only to the plain form of marriage, and you shall recount their particular duties afterwards.

Friar

You come hither, my lord, to marry this lady?

Claudio

No.

Leonato

To be married to her, friar! You come to marry her.

Friar

Lady, you come hither to be married to this count?

Hero

I do.

Friar

If either of you know any inward impediment why you should not be conjoined, I charge you, on your souls, to utter it.

Claudio

Know you any, Hero?

Hero

None, my lord.

Friar

Know you any. Count?

Leonato

I dare make his answer. None.

Claudio

O, what men dare do! What men may do! What men daily do, not knowing what they do!

20. ***Stand thee by*** move aside.
20. ***by your leave*** with your permission.
21. ***unconstrained*** unforced.

25. ***counterpoise*** match.
25. ***render her*** give her back.

28. ***you learn me noble thankfulness*** you teach me the way to show noble gratitude (we can imagine, no doubt, Claudio saying these words with sarcasm or exaggerated politeness, as a contrast with what he is about to do).
30. ***semblance*** appearance, pretence.
31. ***maid*** virgin.
32. ***what authority and show of truth*** what superficial appearance of truth.
34. ***modest evidence*** evidence of (Hero's) modesty.

38. ***luxurious*** lustful.
41. ***knit*** join.
41. ***approved wanton*** proven loose woman.
42. ***proof*** test.

Benedick

How now! Interjections? Why, then, some be of laughing, as, ah, ha, he!

Claudio

Stand thee by, friar. Father, by your leave:
Will you with free and unconstrained soul
Give me this maid, your daughter?

Leonato

As freely, son, as God did give her me.

Claudio

And what have I to give you back whose worth
May counterpoise this rich and precious gift?

Don Pedro

Nothing, unless you render her again.

Claudio

Sweet Prince, you learn me noble thankfulness.
There, Leonato, take her back again;
Give not this rotten orange to your friend;
She's but the sign and semblance of her honour.
Behold how like a maid she blushes here.
O, what authority and show of truth
Can cunning sin cover itself withal!
Comes not that blood as modest evidence
To witness simple virtue? Would you not swear,
All you that see her, that she were a maid
By these exterior shows? But she is none:
She knows the heat of a luxurious bed;
Her blush is guiltiness, not modesty.

Leonato

What do you mean, my lord?

Claudio

Not to be married,
Not to knit my soul to an approved wanton.

Leonato

Dear, my lord, if you, in your own proof,
Have vanquish'd the resistance of her youth,
And made defeat of her virginity –

45. ***known*** had sex with.

47. ***extenuate the 'forehand sin*** excuse the sin of sex before marriage.
49. ***large*** improper.

51. ***comely*** appropriate.

53. ***Out on thee! Seeming!*** Shame on you for pretending.
54. ***Dian*** Diana, goddess of the moon and chastity.
55. ***blown*** fully-bloomed.
56. ***intemperate*** wild, uncontrolled.
57. ***Venus*** goddess of love.

59. ***wide*** mistakenly ('wide of the mark').

62. ***stale*** prostitute.

65. ***nuptial*** wedding.

Claudio
I know what you would say. If I have known her,
You will say she did embrace me as a husband,
And so extenuate the 'forehand sin.
No, Leonato,
I never tempted her with word too large
But, as a brother to his sister, show'd
Bashful sincerity and comely love.

Hero
And seem'd I ever otherwise to you?

Claudio
Out on thee! Seeming! I will write against it.
You seem to me as Dian in her orb,
As chaste as is the bud ere it be blown;
But you are more intemperate in your blood
Than Venus, or those pamp'red animals
That rage in savage sensuality.

Hero
Is my lord well, that he doth speak so wide?

Leonato
Sweet Prince, why speak not you?

Don Pedro
What should I speak?
I stand dishonour'd that have gone about
To link my dear friend to a common stale.

Leonato
Are these things spoken, or do I but dream?

Don John
Sir, they are spoken, and these things are true.

Benedick
This looks not like a nuptial.

Hero
True! O God!

Claudio
Leonato, stand I here?
Is this the Prince? Is this the Prince's brother?
Is this face Hero's? Are our eyes our own?

71. ***kindly power*** natural authority (as her father).

74. ***beset*** attacked.
75. ***catechising*** questioning.

76. ***your name*** In Greek myth, Hero's name meant 'faithful in love'.

78. ***just reproach*** criticism that is fair and proven.

79. ***Hero itself*** the very name, Hero.

81. ***betwixt*** between.

89. ***liberal*** foul-mouthed.

92. ***Fie*** shame.

Leonato
All this is so; but what of this, my lord?
Claudio
Let me but move one question to your daughter;
And, by that fatherly and kindly power
That you have in her, bid her answer truly.
Leonato
I charge thee do so, as thou art my child.
Hero
O, God defend me! how am I beset!
What kind of catechising call you this?
Claudio
To make you answer truly to your name.
Hero
Is it not Hero? Who can blot that name.
With any just reproach?
Claudio
Marry, that can Hero;
Hero itself can blot out Hero's virtue.
What man was he talk'd with you yester-night
Out at your window, betwixt twelve and one?
Now, if you are a maid, answer to this.
Hero
I talk'd with no man at that hour, my lord.
Don Pedro
Why, then are you no maiden. Leonato,
I am sorry you must hear: upon mine honour,
Myself, my brother, and this grieved Count,
Did see her, hear her, at that hour last night,
Talk with a ruffian at her chamber window;
Who hath, indeed, most like a liberal villain,
Confess'd the vile encounters they have had
A thousand times in secret.
Don John
Fie, fie! they are not to be nam'd, my lord,
Not to be spoke of;
There is not chastity enough in language
Without offence to utter them. Thus, pretty lady,

96. ***misgovernment*** misconduct, wrongful behaviour.

101. ***pure impiety and impious purety*** Claudio plays with these oxymorons to emphasise the contrast between Hero's outer pure appearance and behaviour, and her inner 'impiety' – unholy or disrespectful behaviour.

101. ***impious*** unholy, disrespectful.

103. ***conjecture*** suspicion.

109. ***spirits*** senses (here, meaning her consciousness).

I am sorry for thy much misgovernment.

Claudio

O Hero, what a Hero hadst thou been,
If half thy outward graces had been placed
About thy thoughts and counsels of thy heart!
But fare thee well, most foul, most fair! Farewell,
Thou pure impiety and impious purity!
For thee I'll lock up all the gates of love,
And on my eyelids shall conjecture hang,
To turn all beauty into thoughts of harm,
And never shall it more be gracious.

Leonato

Hath no man's dagger here a point for me?

*[*HERO *swoons.]*

Beatrice

Why, how now, cousin! Wherefore sink you down?

Don John

Come, let us go. These things, come thus to light,
Smother her spirits up.

[Exeunt DON PEDRO, DON JOHN, *and* CLAUDIO.*]*

Benedick

How doth the lady?

Beatrice

Dead, I think. Help, uncle!
Hero! why, Hero! Uncle! Signior Benedick! Friar!

Leonato

O Fate, take not away thy heavy hand!
Death is the fairest cover for her shame
That may be wish'd for.

Beatrice

How now, cousin Hero!

Friar

Have comfort, lady.

Leonato

Dost thou look up?

120. ***printed in her blood*** (her guilt) shown by how she is blushing, and a part of her nature. This demonstrates how quickly Leonato, too, is prepared to leap to judgement on Hero – and perhaps doesn't know his daughter as well as we might think. A more generous view would be that the shock of the events have sent him into a sort of hysteria in which he can't see things clearly.
124. ***on the rearward*** immediately after.
126. ***Chid I for that at frugal nature's frame?*** did I complain that Nature only gave me one child?

130. ***issue*** child.
131. ***smirched thus and mir'd with infamy*** stained and muddied with a dreadful reputation.
132. ***part*** blame.
134. ***But mine, and mine I lov'd . . .*** The repetition of 'mine' makes Leonato's speech at this point very touching – the idea that that he, himself, was inextricably linked by love, praise and pride, to Hero, almost as if they were one being.

140. ***salt too little which may season*** the metaphor here refers to there not being enough salt anywhere that would prevent Hero (the 'meat') from 'rotting'. Meat was often salted to prevent it from decaying.

144. ***belied*** falsely accused.

147. ***this twelvemonth*** for the past year.

Friar

Yea; wherefore should she not?

Leonato

Wherefore! Why, doth not every earthly thing
Cry shame upon her? Could she here deny
The story that is printed in her blood?
Do not live, Hero; do not ope thine eyes;
For, did I think thou wouldst not quickly die,
Thought I thy spirits were stronger than thy shames,
Myself would, on the rearward of reproaches,
Strike at thy life. Griev'd I I had but one?
Chid I for that at frugal nature's frame?
O, one too much by thee! Why had I one?
Why ever wast thou lovely in my eyes?
Why had I not, with charitable hand,
Took up a beggar's issue at my gates,
Who smirched thus and mir'd with infamy,
I might have said 'No part of it is mine;
This shame derives itself from unknown loins'?
But mine, and mine I lov'd, and mine I prais'd,
And mine that I was proud on; mine so much
That I myself was to myself not mine,
Valuing of her – why, she, O, she is fall'n
Into a pit of ink, that the wide sea
Hath drops too few to wash her clean again,
And salt too little which may season give
To her foul tainted flesh!

Benedick

Sir, sir, be patient.
For my part, I am so attir'd in wonder,
I know not what to say.

Beatrice

O, on my soul, my cousin is belied!

Benedick

Lady, were you her bedfellow last night?

Beatrice

No, truly not; although, until last night,
I have this twelvemonth been her bedfellow.

156. ***mark'd*** noticed.
157. ***apparitions*** signs.

164. ***Which with experimental seal doth warrant the tenor of my book*** My experience of life backs up what I have learnt and believe to be true.
166. ***divinity*** status as a priest.

171. ***perjury*** lying.

173. ***proper nakedness*** naked truth (i.e uncovered for all to see).

Leonato
Confirm'd, confirm'd! O, that is stronger made
Which was before barr'd up with ribs of iron!
Would the two princes lie; and Claudio lie,
Who lov'd her so, that, speaking of her foulness,
Wash'd it with tears? Hence from her! let her die.

Friar
Hear me a little;
For I have only been silent so long,
And given way unto this course of fortune,
By noting of the lady: I have mark'd
A thousand blushing apparitions
To start into her face, a thousand innocent shames
In angel whiteness beat away those blushes;
And in her eye there hath appear'd a fire
To burn the errors that these princes hold
Against her maiden truth. Call me a fool;
Trust not my reading nor my observations,
Which with experimental seal doth warrant
The tenour of my book; trust not my age,
My reverence, calling, nor divinity,
If this sweet lady lie not guiltless here
Under some biting error.

Leonato
Friar, it cannot be.
Thou seest that all the grace that she hath left
Is that she will not add to her damnation
A sin of perjury; she not denies it.
Why seek'st thou then to cover with excuse
That which appears in proper nakedness?

Friar
Lady, what man is he you are accus'd of?

Hero
They know that do accuse me; I know none.
If I know more of any man alive
Than that which maiden modesty doth warrant
Let all my sins lack mercy! O my father,
Prove you that any man with me convers'd

180. ***unmeet*** inappropriate.

183. ***misprision*** misunderstanding.
184. ***have the very bent of honour*** are honourable in every way.

187. ***toil in frame of villainies*** work to plot wicked deeds.

192. ***invention*** power to plan.
193. ***means*** wealth.
194. ***reft*** robbed.

198. ***To quit me of them thoroughly*** to get them back completely for what they have done.
202. ***publish*** it let it be known.
203. ***mourning ostentation*** outward show of mourning.

206. ***appertain*** relate.

At hours unmeet, or that I yesternight
Maintain'd the change of words with any creature,
Refuse me, hate me, torture me to death.

Friar

There is some strange misprision in the princes.

Benedick

Two of them have the very bent of honour;
And if their wisdoms be misled in this,
The practice of it lives in John the bastard,
Whose spirits toil in frame of villainies.

Leonato

I know not. If they speak but truth of her,
These hands shall tear her; if they wrong her honour,
The proudest of them shall well hear of it.
Time hath not yet so dried this blood of mine,
Nor age so eat up my invention,
Nor fortune made such havoc of my means,
Nor my bad life reft me so much of friends,
But they shall find awak'd in such a kind
Both strength of limb and policy of mind,
Ability in means and choice of friends,
To quit me of them throughly.

Friar

Pause awhile,
And let my counsel sway you in this case.
Your daughter here the princes left for dead;
Let her awhile be secretly kept in,
And publish it that she is dead indeed;
Maintain a mourning ostentation,
And on your family's old monument
Hang mournful epitaphs, and do all rites
That appertain unto a burial.

Leonato

What shall become of this? What will this do?

Friar

Marry, this, well carried, shall on her behalf
Change slander to remorse; that is some good.
But not for that dream I on this strange course,

211. ***on this travail*** from these things you have to do.

216. ***prize not to the worth*** do not appreciate.

218. ***rack*** exaggerate.

220. ***fare*** happen.

223. ***study of imagination*** reflective thoughts.
224. ***organ of her life*** aspect of her beauty.
225. ***apparell'd*** dressed.
225. ***habit*** clothing.
226. ***delicate*** graceful.

228. ***liver*** believed by the Elizabethans to be the source of love.

235. ***if all aim but this be levelled false*** if the rest of my plan should fail.

237. ***quench the wonder of her infamy*** silence the gossip about her.
238. ***sort*** turn out.

243. ***inwardness*** close friendship.

But on this travail look for greater birth.
She dying, as it must be so maintained,
Upon the instant that she was accus'd,
Shall be lamented, pitied, and excus'd,
Of every hearer; for it so falls out
That what we have we prize not to the worth
Whiles we enjoy it, but being lack'd and lost,
Why, then we rack the value, then we find
The virtue that possession would not show us
Whiles it was ours. So will it fare with Claudio.
When he shall hear she died upon his words,
Th' idea of her life shall sweetly creep
Into his study of imagination,
And every lovely organ of her life
Shall come apparell'd in more precious habit,
More moving, delicate, and full of life,
Into the eye and prospect of his soul,
Than when she liv'd indeed. Then shall he mourn,
If ever love had interest in his liver,
And wish he had not so accused her –
No, though he thought his accusation true.
Let this be so, and doubt not but success
Will fashion the event in better shape
Than I can lay it down in likelihood.
But if all aim but this be levell'd false,
The supposition of the lady's death
Will quench the wonder other infamy.
And if it sort not well, you may conceal her,
As best befits her wounded reputation,
In some reclusive and religious life,
Out of all eyes, tongues, minds, and injuries.

Benedick

Signior Leonato, let the friar advise you;
And though you know my inwardness and love
Is very much unto the Prince and Claudio,
Yet, by mine honour, I will deal in this
As secretly and justly as your soul
Should with your body.

248. ***twine*** thin cord or string.

250. ***strange sores strangely they strain the cure*** a desperate disease must have a desperate cure.

252. ***prolong'd*** postponed, put off.

259. ***right her*** prove her innocence.

261. ***even*** straightforward.

263. ***office*** task.

Leonato

Being that I flow in grief
The smallest twine may lead me.

Friar

'Tis well consented. Presently away;
For to strange sores strangely they strain the cure.
Come, lady, die to live; this wedding day
Perhaps is but prolong'd; have patience and endure.

[Exeunt all but BENEDICK *and* BEATRICE.*]*

Benedick

Lady Beatrice, have you wept all this while?

Beatrice

Yea, and I will weep a while longer.

Benedick

I will not desire that.

Beatrice

You have no reason; I do it freely.

Benedick

Surely I do believe your fair cousin is wronged.

Beatrice

Ah, how much might the man deserve of me that would right her!

Benedick

Is there any way to show such friendship?

Beatrice

A very even way, but no such friend.

Benedick

May a man do it?

Beatrice

It is a man's office, but not yours.

Benedick

I do love nothing in the world so well as you. Is not that strange?

Beatrice

As strange as the thing I know not. It were as possible for me to say I lov'd nothing so well as you; but believe me not, and yet I lie not; I confess

273. ***eat it*** take it back.

275. ***protest*** swear.

279. ***stayed me in a happy hour*** found me at a fortunate moment.

288. ***Tarry*** wait.

nothing, nor I deny nothing. I am sorry for my cousin.

Benedick

By my sword, Beatrice, thou lovest me.

Beatrice

Do not swear, and eat it.

Benedick

I will swear by it that you love me; and I will make him eat it that says I love not you.

Beatrice

Will you not eat your word?

Benedick

With no sauce that can be devised to it; I protest I love thee.

Beatrice

Why, then, God forgive me!

Benedick

What offence, sweet Beatrice?

Beatrice

You have stayed me in a happy hour; I was about to protest I loved you.

Benedick

And do it with all thy heart?

Beatrice

I love you with so much of my heart that none is left to protest.

Benedick

Come, bid me do anything for thee.

Beatrice

Kill Claudio.

Benedick

Ha! not for the wide world.

Beatrice

You kill me to deny it. Farewell.

Benedick

Tarry, sweet Beatrice.

297. ***Is 'a not*** is he not.
297. ***approved in the height*** shown to be the greatest.
298. ***kinswoman*** family member.
299. ***bear her in hand*** lead her on.
300. ***take hands*** marry.
301. ***unmitigated rancour*** uncontrolled hatred.

305. ***proper saying*** likely story.

308. ***undone*** ruined.

310. ***Counties*** counts.
311. ***Comfect*** Candy.

Beatrice

I am gone though I am here; there is no love in you; nay, I pray you, let me go.

Benedick

Beatrice –

Beatrice

In faith, I will go.

Benedick

We'll be friends first.

Beatrice

You dare easier be friends with me than fight with mine enemy.

Benedick

Is Claudio thine enemy?

Beatrice

Is 'a not approved in the height a villain that hath slandered, scorned, dishonoured, my kinswoman? O that I were a man! What! bear her in hand until they come to take hands, and then with public accusation, uncovered slander, unmitigated rancour – O God, that I were a man! I would eat his heart in the market-place.

Benedick

Hear me, Beatrice.

Beatrice

Talk with a man out at a window! A proper saying!

Benedick

Nay, but, Beatrice –

Beatrice

Sweet Hero! She is wrong'd, she is sland'red, she is undone.

Benedick

Beat –

Beatrice

Princes and Counties! Surely, a princely testimony, a goodly count. Count Comfect; a sweet gallant, surely! O that I were a man for his sake! or that I had any friend would be a man for my sake! But

315. ***curtsies*** courtly manners.

328. ***render me a dear account*** pay dearly for what he's done.

manhood is melted into curtsies, valour into compliment, and men are only turn'd into tongue, and trim ones too. He is now as valiant as Hercules that only tells a lie and swears it. I cannot be a man with wishing, therefore I will die a woman with grieving.

Benedick

Tarry, good Beatrice. By this hand, I love thee.

Beatrice

Use it for my love some other way than swearing by it.

Benedick

Think you in your soul the Count Claudio hath wrong'd Hero?

Beatrice

Yea, as sure as I have a thought or a soul.

Benedick

Enough, I am engag'd; I will challenge him; I will kiss your hand, and so I leave you. By this hand, Claudio shall render me a dear account. As you hear of me, so think of me. Go comfort your cousin; I must say she is dead; and so, farewell.

[Exeunt.]

SCENE II

This scene reveals Don John's deception in more detail, and begins the process of resolving the problems it has caused. Whilst there is comedy to be found in Dogberry's misuse of words and phrases, and in his own inflated view of himself, the key sense the audience is left with is that things are coming to a head, and that whilst harmony is not yet restored, there is now a chance that it will be.

2. ***dissembly*** Dogberry means 'assembly'.

2. ***sexton*** person employed by the church to carry out various duties.

3. ***malefactors*** offenders.

12. ***sirrah*** fellow.

18. ***defend*** forbid.

Scene II

A prison.

[Enter DOGBERRY, VERGES, *and* SEXTON, *in gowns; and the* WATCH, *with* CONRADE *and* BORACHIO.*]*

Dogberry
Is our whole dissembly appear'd?

Verges
O, a stool and a cushion for the sexton!

Sexton
Which be the malefactors?

Dogberry
Marry, that am I and my partner.

Verges
Nay, that's certain; we have the exhibition to examine.

Sexton
But which are the offenders that are to be examin'd? Let them come before Master Constable.

Dogberry
Yea, marry, let them come before me. What is your name, friend?

Borachio
Borachio.

Dogberry
Pray write down Borachio. Yours, sirrah?

Conrade
I am a gentleman, sir, and my name is Conrade.

Dogberry
Write down Master Gentleman Conrade. Masters, do you serve God?

Conrade, Borachio
Yea, sir, we hope.

Dogberry
Write down that they hope they serve God; and write God first; for God defend but God should go before

20. ***knaves*** rogues.
20–21. ***it will go near to be thought so shortly*** it will be believed more generally soon.

24–5. ***go about with*** deal with.

29. ***in a tale*** telling the same story.

31. ***go not the way to examine*** are not following the correct procedure.

34. ***eftest*** an invented word, probably meaning 'aptest' or easiest.
35. ***charge*** command.

such villains! Masters, it is proved already that you are little better than false knaves, and it will go near to be thought so shortly. How answer you for yourselves?

Conrade

Marry, sir, we say we are none.

Dogberry

A marvellous witty fellow, I assure you; but I will go about with him. Come you hither, sirrah; a word in your ear: sir, I say to you it is thought you are false knaves.

Borachio

Sir, I say to you we are none.

Dogberry

Well, stand aside. Fore God, they are both in a tale. Have you writ down that they are none?

Sexton

Master Constable, you go not the way to examine; you must call forth the watch that are their accusers.

Dogberry

Yea, marry, that's the eftest way. Let the watch come forth. Masters, I charge you in the Prince's name, accuse these men.

1 Watch

This man said, sir, that Don John, the Prince's brother, was a villain.

Dogberry

Write down Prince John a villain. Why, this is flat perjury, to call a prince's brother villain.

Borachio

Master Constable – Dogberry Pray thee, fellow, peace; I do not like thy look, I promise thee.

Sexton

What heard you him say else?

2 Watch

Marry, that he had received a thousand ducats of Don John for accusing the Lady Hero wrongfully.

46. ***flat burglary*** downright theft (nothing to do with apartments!).

52. ***redemption*** means, literally, the act of being redeemed or saved, but in fact Dogberry means the opposite – 'damnation'!

59. ***refus'd*** disowned, rejected.

63. ***opinion'd*** Dogberry means 'pinioned' – tied up (so they can't escape).

67. ***coxcomb*** a vain fool.
68. ***naughty varlet*** wicked rascal.

Dogberry
Flat burglary as ever was committed.

Verges
Yea, by mass, that it is.

Sexton
What else, fellow?

1 Watch
And that Count Claudio did mean, upon his words, to disgrace Hero before the whole assembly, and not marry her.

Dogberry
O villain! thou wilt be condemn'd into everlasting redemption for this.

Sexton
What else?

2 Watch
This is all.

Sexton
And this is more, masters, than you can deny. Prince John is this morning secretly stol'n away; Hero was in this manner accus'd, in this very manner refus'd and upon the grief of this suddenly died. Master Constable, let these men be bound and brought to Leonato's; I will go before and show him their examination.

[Exit.]

Dogberry
Come, let them be opinion'd.

Verges
Let them be in the hands.

Conrade
Off, coxcomb.

Dogberry
God's my life, where's the sexton? Let him write down the Prince's officer coxcomb. Come, bind them. Thou naughty varlet!

70. ***suspect my place*** Dogberry means 'respect' his position.

72–3. ***remember that I am an ass*** Dogberry is keen that the insult he has been called is written down somewhere as evidence against Conrade, but in so doing he manages to make it sound as if wants to be called an 'ass'!

Conrade

Away! you are an ass, you are an ass.

Dogberry

Dost thou not suspect my place? Dost thou not suspect my years? O that he were here to write me down an ass! But, masters, remember that I am an ass; though it be not written down, yet forget not that I am an ass. No, thou villain, thou art full of piety, as shall be prov'd upon thee by good witness. I am a wise fellow; and, which is more, an officer; and, which is more, a householder; and, which is more, as pretty a piece of flesh as any is in Messina; and one that knows the law, go to; and a rich fellow enough, go to; and a fellow that hath had losses; and one that hath two gowns, and everything handsome about him. Bring him away. O that I had been writ down an ass!

[Exeunt.]

ACT V SCENE 1

The drama in this scene comes in the fall from grace of Don Pedro and Claudio. The scene begins with them mocking Benedick and laughing at his challenge. When the truth about Don John's villainy is revealed, Claudio says 'I have drunk poison . . .', meaning that as he heard the truth it felt like poison was going through his body. By the end they are ready to accept any penance that Leonato is willing to propose. Dramatic irony is very much at work here; while Claudio and Don Pedro laugh and joke at Benedick's expense, we know their comedy is hollow, and that the ticking time-bomb of what really happened will soon 'go off'.
2 ***second*** reinforce.

3. ***counsel*** advice.
4. ***profitless*** useless.

7. ***do suit with*** are equal to.

14. ***lineament*** element.
16. ***wag*** fool.
16. ***cry*** 'hem' clear the throat, as before a speech.
17. ***patch grief with proverbs*** patch up his wounds with moral sayings.
17. ***make misfortune drunk*** drown sorrows.
18. ***candle-wasters*** scholars, i.e. Leonato means drown sorrows by thinking and reflecting.

24. ***preceptial medicine*** helpful guidance.
25. ***fetter*** hold back.

ACT FIVE
Scene I

Before Leonato's house.

[Enter LEONATO *and* ANTONIO.*]*

Antonio

If you go on thus, you will kill yourself,
And 'tis not wisdom thus to second grief
Against yourself.

Leonato

I pray thee cease thy counsel,
Which falls into mine ears as profitless
As water in a sieve. Give not me counsel
Nor let no comforter delight mine ear
But such a one whose wrongs do suit with mine.
Bring me a father that so lov'd his child,
Whose joy of her is overwhelm'd like mine,
And bid him speak of patience;
Measure his woe the length and breadth of mine,
And let it answer every strain for strain;
As thus for thus, and such a grief for such,
In every lineament, branch, shape, and form.
If such a one will smile and stroke his beard,
And sorrow wag, cry 'hem!' when he should groan,
Patch grief with proverbs, make misfortune drunk
With candle-wasters – bring him yet to me,
And I of him will gather patience.
But there is no such man; for, brother, men
Can counsel and speak comfort to that grief
Which they themselves not feel; but, tasting it,
Their counsel turns to passion, which before
Would give preceptial medicine to rage,
Fetter strong madness in a silken thread,
Charm ache with air and agony with words.
No, no; 'tis all men's office to speak patience

28. ***wring*** writhe.

32. ***advertisement*** good advice.

37. ***writ the style of gods*** assumed a god-like tone.
38. ***made a push at*** scorned, or defied.

42. ***belied*** falsely accused.

46. ***Good den*** good evening.

48. ***We have some haste*** we are in a hurry (where might Don Pedro and Claudio be hurrying to? Are they leaving – or just trying to avoid an unpleasant conversation with Leonato?).
50. ***all is one*** never mind.

To those that wring under the load of sorrow,
But no man's virtue nor sufficiency
To be so moral when he shall endure
The like himself. Therefore, give me no counsel;
My griefs cry louder than advertisement.

Antonio
Therein do men from children nothing differ.

Leonato
I pray thee peace; I will be flesh and blood;
For there was never yet philosopher
That could endure the toothache patiently,
However they have writ the style of gods,
And made a push at chance and sufferance.

Antonio
Yet bend not all the harm upon yourself;
Make those that do offend you suffer too.

Leonato
There thou speak'st reason; nay, I will do so.
My soul doth tell me Hero is belied;
And that shall Claudio know; so shall the Prince,
And all of them that thus dishonour her.

Antonio
Here comes the Prince and Claudio hastily.

[*Enter* DON PEDRO *and* CLAUDIO.]

Don Pedro
Good den, good den.

Claudio
Good day to both of you.

Leonato
Hear you, my lords!

Don Pedro
We have some haste, Leonato.

Leonato
Some haste, my lord! Well, fare you well, my lord.
Are you so hasty now? Well, all is one.

Don Pedro
Nay, do not quarrel with us, good old man.

54 ***dissembler*** deceiver.

56. ***beshrew*** curse.

59. ***fleer*** scorn.
60. ***dotard*** senile old man.

63. ***to thy head*** to your face.

65. ***reverence*** by respect (for you) to one side.

67. ***trial of a man*** single combat/duel.

72. ***fram'd*** the result of.

76. ***nice fence*** skilful sword-play.

Antonio
If he could right himself with quarrelling,
Some of us would lie low.

Claudio
Who wrongs him?

Leonato
Marry, thou dost wrong me; thou dissembler, thou!
Nay, never lay thy hand upon thy sword;
I fear thee not.

Claudio
Marry, beshrew my hand
If it should give your age such cause of fear!
In faith, my hand meant nothing to my sword.

Leonato
Tush, tush, man; never fleer and jest at me;
I speak not like a dotard nor a fool,
As under privilege of age to brag
What I have done being young, or what would do
Were I not old. Know, Claudio, to thy head,
Thou hast so wrong'd mine innocent child and me
That I am forc'd to lay my reverence by,
And with grey hairs and bruise of many days
Do challenge thee to trial of a man.
I say thou hast belied mine innocent child;
Thy slander hath gone through and through her heart,
And she lies buried with her ancestors –
O! in a tomb where never scandal slept,
Save this of hers, fram'd by thy villainy.

Claudio
My villainy!

Leonato
Thine, Claudio; thine, I say.

Don Pedro
You say not right, old man.

Leonato
My lord, my lord,
I'll prove it on his body if he dare,
Despite his nice fence and his active practice,

77. ***May of youth*** meaning in the Spring (the freshest time) of his youth, and therefore at his most energetic.
77. ***lustihood*** physical fitness.

79. ***daff me*** brush me aside.

84. ***answer me*** respond to my challenge.

86. ***foining*** a fencing move.

93. ***apes*** fools.
93. ***Jacks*** rogues, villains.
93. ***milksops*** feeble young men.

95. ***utmost scruple*** smallest amount.
96. ***Scambling*** rough, uncontrolled.
96. ***out-facing*** conceited.
96. ***fashion-monging boys*** superficial followers of fashion.
97. ***cog*** cheat.
97. ***flout*** brag, boast.
97. ***deprave*** bring down.
98. ***Go anticly*** dress grotesquely, strangely.
100. ***durst*** dare to.

103. ***meddle*** interrupt.

His May of youth and bloom of lustihood.
Claudio
Away! I will not have to do with you.
Leonato
Canst thou so daff me?
Thou hast kill'd my child;
If thou kill'st me, boy, thou shalt kill a man.
Antonio
He shall kill two of us, and men indeed;
But that's no matter; let him kill one first.
Win me and wear me; let him answer me.
Come, follow me, boy; come, sir boy, come follow me;
Sir boy, I'll whip you from your foining fence;
Nay, as I am a gentleman, I will.
Leonato
Brother –
Antonio
Content yourself. God knows I lov'd my niece;
And she is dead, slander'd to death by villains,
That dare as well answer a man indeed
As I dare take a serpent by the tongue.
Boys, apes, braggarts. Jacks, milksops!
Leonato
Brother Antony –
Antonio
Hold you content. What, man! I know them, yea,
And what they weigh, even to the utmost scruple –
Scambling, out-facing, fashion-monging boys,
That lie and cog and flout, deprave and slander,
Go anticly, and show outward hideousness,
And speak off half a dozen dang'rous words,
How they might hurt their enemies, if they durst;
And this is all.
Leonato
But, brother Antony –
Antonio
Come, 'tis no matter;
Do not you meddle; let me deal in this.

115. *fray* brawl, battle.

119. ***I doubt*** I am afraid.

Don Pedro
Gentlemen both, we will not wake your patience.
My heart is sorry for your daughter's death;
But, on my honour, she was charg'd with nothing
But what was true, and very full of proof.

Leonato
My lord, my lord –

Don Pedro
I will not hear you.

Leonato
No? Come, brother, away. I will be heard.

Antonio
And shall, or some of us will smart for it.

[*Exeunt* LEONATO *and* ANTONIO.]

Don Pedro
See, see; here comes the man we went to seek.

[*Enter* BENEDICK.]

Claudio
Now, signior, what news?

Benedick
Good day, my lord.

Don Pedro
Welcome, signior; you are almost come to part almost a fray.

Claudio
We had lik'd to have had our two noses snapp'd off with two old men without teeth.

Don Pedro
Leonato and his brother. What think'st thou? Had we fought, I doubt we should have been too young for them.

Benedick
In a false quarrel there is no true valour. I came to seek you both.

124. ***high-proof*** extremely.

126. ***scabbard*** sword-holder.

133. ***care kill'd a cat*** a proverb – worrying too much isn't good for you career process (is Benedick also turning the word 'care' back on Claudio?).
135–6. ***charge it*** use it.

141. ***knows how to turn his girdle*** what to do about it.

Claudio

We have been up and down to seek thee; for we are high-proof melancholy, and would fain have it beaten away. Wilt thou use thy wit?

Benedick

It is in my scabbard; shall I draw it?

Don Pedro

Dost thou wear thy wit by thy side?

Claudio

Never any did so, though very many have been beside their wit. I will bid thee draw, as we do the minstrels – draw to pleasure us.

Don Pedro

As I am an honest man, he looks pale. Art thou sick or angry?

Claudio

What, courage, man! What though care kill'd a cat, thou hast mettle enough in thee to kill care.

Benedick

Sir, I shall meet your wit in the career, an you charge it against me. I pray you choose another subject.

Claudio

Nay, then, give him another staff; this last was broke cross.

Don Pedro

By this light, he changes more and more; I think he be angry indeed.

Claudio

If he be, he knows how to turn his girdle.

Benedick

Shall I speak a word in your ear?

Claudio

God bless me from a challenge!

Benedick

[Aside to CLAUDIO*]* You are a villain; I jest not; I will make it good how you dare, with what you dare, and when you dare. Do me right, or I will protest

146. ***protest*** declare.
148. ***fall heavy*** bring punishment.
148–9. ***Let me hear from you*** So, what do you have to say for yourself?

152–5. ***calf . . . capon . . . woodcock*** (considered) foolish animals.

154. ***curiously*** skilfully.

158. ***fine*** delicate.

160. ***gross*** fat.
162. ***wise gentleman*** meant sarcastically, or ironically – in other words, a fool.
163. ***hath the tongues*** is a linguist.
165. ***forswore*** took back.

167. ***trans-shape*** distort.

169. ***proper'st*** most handsome.

173. ***deadly*** until she died.

your cowardice. You have kill'd a sweet lady, and her death shall fall heavy on you. Let me hear from you.

Claudio

Well, I will meet you, so I may have good cheer.

Don Pedro

What, a feast? a feast?

Claudio

I' faith, I thank him; he hath bid me to a calf's head and a capon, the which if I do not carve most curiously, say my knife's naught. Shall I not find a woodcock too?

Benedick

Sir, your wit ambles well; it goes easily.

Don Pedro

I'll tell thee how Beatrice prais'd thy wit the other day. I said thou hadst a fine wit. True,' said she 'a fine little one.' 'No,' said I 'a great wit.' 'Right,' says she 'a great gross one.' 'Nay,' said I 'a good wit.' 'Just,' said she 'it hurts nobody.' 'Nay,' said I 'the gentleman is wise.' 'Certain,' said she 'a wise gentleman.' 'Nay/ said I 'he hath the tongues.' That I believe,' said she 'for he swore a thing to me on Monday night, which he forswore on Tuesday morning. There's a double tongue; there's two tongues.' Thus did she, an hour together, trans-shape thy particular virtues; yet, at last, she concluded, with a sigh, thou wast the proper'st man in Italy.

Claudio

For the which she wept heartily, and said she cared not.

Don Pedro

Yea, that she did; but yet, for all that, an if she did not hate him deadly, she would love him dearly. The old man's daughter told us all.

Claudio

All, all; and, moreover, 'God saw him when he was hid in the garden'.

177–8. ***set the savage bull's horns on the sensible Benedick's head*** see you married (with a reference, perhaps, to husbands being 'cuckolds' – with wives who are unfaithful, so also an insult).

183. ***braggarts*** boasting lads

185–6. ***I must discontinue your company*** I resign from your service (it seems Benedick is less angry with Don Pedro, thanking him for his 'many courtesies').

190. ***in earnest serious*** (is Don Pedro beginning to suspect for the first time that things are not quite as they appear?).

195–6. ***goes in his doublet and hose*** takes off his cloak to prepare for a fight.

197. ***giant to an ape*** even larger than an ape.
197–8. ***a doctor*** superior in intelligence.

199–200. ***be sad*** be serious (for a moment).

Don Pedro

But when shall we set the savage bull's horns on the sensible Benedick's head?

Claudio

Yea, and text underneath, 'Here dwells Benedick the married man'?

Benedick

Fare you well, boy; you know my mind. I will leave you now to your gossip-like humour; you break jests as braggarts do their blades, which. God be thanked, hurt not. My lord, for your many courtesies I thank you. I must discontinue your company. Your brother the bastard is fled from Messina. You have among you kill'd a sweet and innocent lady. For my Lord Lackbeard there, he and I shall meet; and till then, peace be with him.

[*Exit* BENEDICK.]

Don Pedro

He is in earnest.

Claudio

In most profound earnest; and I'll warrant you for the love of Beatrice.

Don Pedro

And hath challeng'd thee?

Claudio

Most sincerely.

Don Pedro

What a pretty thing man is when he goes in his doublet and hose and leaves off his wit!

Claudio

He is then a giant to an ape; but then is an ape a doctor to such a man.

Don Pedro

But, soft you, let me be; pluck up, my heart, and be sad. Did he not say my brother was fled?

[*Enter* DOGBERRY, VERGES, *and the* WATCH, *with* CONRADE *and* BORACHIO.]

202. ***ne'er weigh more reasons in her balance*** never again weigh up the evidence (Justice was generally signified by a pair of scales)
203. ***cursing hypocrite*** lying imposter.

207. ***Hearken*** after enquire about.

218. ***in his own division*** in his own way of speaking (Claudio is referring to the deliberately confused way Don Pedro has answered Dogberry).

221. ***bound to your answer*** called to answer charges.
222. ***cunning*** clever.
223–36. ***Sweet Prince . . . reward of a villain*** On the surface, it seems strange that Borachio should so willingly confess his crimes, given the lack of intelligence of Dogberry and co, but perhaps it can be explained in his words when he says, 'The lady is dead upon mine and my master's false accusation . . .', suggesting that for him it was a nasty trick that got terribly out of hand. Furthermore, Don John has now fled from Messina, suggesting that Borachio will have to face the music alone. Perhaps he sees no reason now for hiding Don John's part in it all.

Dogberry

Come, you, sir; if justice cannot tame you, she shall ne'er weigh more reasons in her balance; nay, an you be a cursing hypocrite once, you must be look'd to.

Don Pedro

How now! two of my brother's men bound – Borachio one.

Claudio

Hearken after their offence, my lord.

Don Pedro

Officers, what offence have these men done?

Dogberry

Marry, sir, they have committed false report; moreover, they have spoken untruths; secondarily, they are slanders; sixth and lastly, they have belied a lady; thirdly, they have verified unjust things; and to conclude, they are lying knaves.

Don Pedro

First, I ask thee what they have done; thirdly, I ask thee what's their offence; sixth and lastly, why they are committed; and to conclude, what you lay to their charge.

Claudio

Rightly reasoned, and in his own division; and, by my troth, there's one meaning well suited.

Don Pedro

Who have you offended, masters, that you are thus bound to your answer? This learned constable is too cunning to be understood. What's your offence?

Borachio

Sweet Prince, let me go no farther to mine answer; do you hear me, and let this Count kill me. I have deceived even your very eyes. What your wisdoms could not discover, these shallow fools have brought to light; who, in the night, overheard me confessing to this man how Don John your brother incensed me to slander the Lady Hero; how you were brought into the

230–1. ***court Margaret*** flirt with and behave lovingly towards Margaret.

239. ***set thee on to this*** urge you to do this.

244. ***rare semblance*** especially beautiful appearance.

252. ***note*** see (remember the reference to 'note' related to 'noting/nothing' which has cropped up throughout the play – the theme of what you see and what is the truth behind it).

orchard, and saw me court Margaret in Hero's garments; how you disgrac'd her, when you should marry her. My villainy they have upon record; which I had rather seal with my death than repeat over to my shame. The lady is dead upon mine and my master's false accusation; and, briefly, I desire nothing but the reward of a villain.

Don Pedro
Runs not this speech like iron through your blood?

Claudio
I have drunk poison whiles he utter'd it.

Don Pedro
But did my brother set thee on to this?

Borachio
Yea, and paid me richly for the practice of it.

Don Pedro
He is compos'd and fram'd of treachery,
And fled he is upon this villainy.

Claudio
Sweet Hero, now thy image doth appear
In the rare semblance that I lov'd it first.

Dogberry
Come, bring away the plaintiffs; by this time our sexton hath reformed Signior Leonato of the matter. And, masters, do not forget to specify, when time and place shall serve, that I am an ass.

Verges
Here, here comes Master Signior Leonato and the sexton too.

[Re-enter LEONATO *and* ANTONIO, *with the* SEXTON.*]*

Leonato
Which is the villain? Let me see his eyes,
That when I note another man like him
I may avoid him. Which of these is he?

Borachio
If you would know your wronger, look on me.

257. ***beliest thyself*** wrong yourself.

262. ***bethink you of it*** think about it.

265. ***penance*** punishment.

270. ***enjoin*** commit.

273. ***Possess*** inform, tell.

273. ***labour aught in sad invention*** write a sad poem.

283. ***Give her the right*** i.e. marry her.

Leonato

Art thou the slave that with thy breath hast kill'd
Mine innocent child?

Borachio

Yea, even I alone.

Leonato

No, not so, villain; thou beliest thyself;
Here stand a pair of honourable men,
A third is fled, that had a hand in it.
I thank you, princes, for my daughter's death;
Record it with your high and worthy deeds;
'Twas bravely done, if you bethink you of it.

Claudio

I know not how to pray your patience,
Yet I must speak. Choose your revenge yourself;
Impose me to what penance your invention
Can lay upon my sin; yet sinn'd I not
But in mistaking.

Don Pedro

By my soul, nor I;
And yet, to satisfy this good old man,
I would bend under any heavy weight
That he'll enjoin me to.

Leonato

I cannot bid you bid my daughter live –
That were impossible; but, I pray you both,
Possess the people in Messina here
How innocent she died; and, if your love
Can labour aught in sad invention,
Hang her an epitaph upon her tomb,
And sing it to her bones; sing it to-night.
To-morrow morning come you to my house;
And since you could not be my son-in-law,
Be yet my nephew. My brother hath a daughter,
Almost the copy of my child that's dead;
And she alone is heir to both of us.
Give her the right you should have giv'n her cousin,
And so dies my revenge.

286. ***embrace*** gladly accept.
287. ***dispose for henceforth*** do what you like with/to me from now on.

289. ***naughty*** wicked.

291. ***pack'd in*** an accomplice to.

296–7. ***under white and black*** recorded in writing.

301–2. ***borrows money in God's name*** begs for money.

310. ***God save the foundation!*** this is how the poor might respond to a charitable donation or gift of money.

Claudio

O noble sir!
Your over-kindness doth wring tears from me.
I do embrace your offer; and dispose
For henceforth of poor Claudio.

Leonato

To-morrow, then, I will expect your coming;
To-night I take my leave. This naughty man
Shall face to face be brought to Margaret,
Who, I believe, was pack'd in all this wrong,
Hir'd to it by your brother.

Borachio

No, by my soul, she was not;
Nor knew not what she did when she spoke to me;
But always hath been just and virtuous
In anything that I do know by her.

Dogberry

Moreover, sir, which indeed is not under white and black, this plaintiff here, the offender, did call me ass; I beseech you, let it be rememb'red in his punishment. And also, the watch heard them talk of one Deformed; they say he wears a key in his ear and a lock hanging by it, and borrows money in God's name; the which he hath us'd so long, and never paid, that now men grow hard-hearted, and will lend nothing for God's sake. Pray you examine him upon that point.

Leonato

I thank thee for thy care and honest pains.

Dogberry

Your worship speaks like a most thankful and reverend youth, and I praise God for you.

Leonato

There's for thy pains.

Dogberry

God save the foundation!

Leonato

Go; I discharge thee of thy prisoner, and I thank thee.

320. ***look for you*** will expect you.

325. ***lewd*** worthless.

Dogberry

I leave an arrant knave with your worship; which I beseech your worship to correct yourself, for the example of others. God keep your worship! I wish your worship well; God restore you to health! I humbly give you leave to depart; and if a merry meeting may be wish'd. God prohibit it! Come, neighbour.

[Exeunt DOGBERRY *and* VERGES.*]*

Leonato

Until to-morrow morning, lords, farewell.

Antonio

Farewell, my lords; we look for you to-morrow.

Don Pedro

We will not fail.

Claudio

To-night I'll mourn with Hero.

[Exeunt DON PEDRO *and* CLAUDIO.*]*

Leonato

[To the WATCH*]* Bring you these fellows on. We'll talk with Margaret
How her acquaintance grew with this lewd fellow.

[Exeunt severally.]

SCENE II

This short scene serves to emphasise the developing relationship between Beatrice and Benedick. They are alone here and, unassisted, declare their feelings for each other. The scene also allows Ursula to sum up for the audience what has recently happened; she explains that Hero was falsely accused and that Claudio and Don Pedro were tricked.

1–2. ***deserve well at my hands*** earn my thanks.

5. ***high*** formal, decorative.
6. ***comely*** pleasing.

9. ***keep below stairs*** remain a servant.

15–16. ***give thee the bucklers*** admit defeat.

Scene II

Leonato's orchard.

[Enter BENEDICK *and* MARGARET, *meeting.]*

Benedick

Pray thee, sweet Mistress Margaret, deserve well at my hands by helping me to the speech of Beatrice.

Margaret

Will you then write me a sonnet in praise of my beauty?

Benedick

In so high a style, Margaret, that no man living shall come over it; for, in most comely truth, thou deservest it.

Margaret

To have no man come over me! Why, shall I always keep below stairs?

Benedick

Thy wit is as quick as the greyhound's mouth; it catches.

Margaret

And yours as blunt as the fencer's foils, which hit, but hurt not.

Benedick

A most manly wit, Margaret; it will not hurt a woman; and so, I pray thee, call Beatrice. I give thee the bucklers.

Margaret

Give us the swords; we have bucklers of our own.

Benedick

If you use them, Margaret, you must put in the pikes with a vice; and they are dangerous weapons for maids.

Margaret

Well, I will call Beatrice to you, who, I think, hath legs.

28. ***Leander*** a hero of Greek myth, who drowned trying to swim to his love, Hero (ironically).
29. ***Troilus*** a Trojan prince who found a way of seeing his faithless love, Cressida, through her uncle.
29. ***panders*** go-betweens.
30. ***quondam carpet-mongers*** former romantic lovers.
32. ***blank verse*** unrhymed.

38–9. ***I cannot woo in festival terms*** I can't compose love poetry.

46. ***that I came*** what I came for.

[*Exit* MARGARET.]

Benedick

And therefore will come.

[*Sings.*]

The god of love,
That sits above,
And knows me, and knows me,
How pitiful I deserve –

I mean in singing; but in loving – Leander the good swimmer, Troilus the first employer of panders, and a whole bookful of these quondam carpet-mongers, whose names yet run smoothly in the even road of a blank verse, why, they were never so truly turn'd over and over as my poor self in love. Marry, I cannot show it in rhyme; I have tried; I can find out no rhyme to 'lady' but 'baby' – an innocent rhyme; for 'scorn', 'horn' – a hard rhyme; for 'school', 'fool' – a babbling rhyme; very ominous endings. No, I was not born under a rhyming planet, nor I cannot woo in festival terms.

[*Enter* BEATRICE.]

Sweet Beatrice, wouldst thou come when I call'd thee?

Beatrice

Yea, signior, and depart when you bid me.

Benedick

O, stay but till then!

Beatrice

'Then' is spoken; fare you well now. And yet, ere I go, let me go with that I came, which is, with knowing what hath pass'd between you and Claudio.

Benedick

Only foul words; and thereupon I will kiss thee.

51. ***noisome*** unpleasant.

55. ***undergoes*** takes up.
56. ***subscribe*** proclaim.

59. ***politic*** sensible.
60. ***admit*** allow.

63. ***epithet*** a word or short phrase used to describe someone or something.

71. ***instance*** truth.
71–2. ***the time of good neighbours*** the past.
72–5. ***if a man do not erect . . . widow weeps*** if a man does not build a memorial to himself before he dies, he will only be remembered for as long as his burial service lasts.

77. ***Question*** Good question!
77. ***clamour*** noise.

Beatrice

Foul words is but foul wind, and foul wind is but foul breath, and foul breath is noisome; therefore I will depart unkiss'd.

Benedick

Thou hast frighted the word out of his right sense, so forcible is thy wit. But, I must tell thee plainly, Claudio undergoes my challenge; and either I must shortly hear from him, or I will subscribe him a coward. And, I pray thee now, tell me for which of my bad parts didst thou first fall in love with me?

Beatrice

For them all together; which maintain'd so politic a state of evil that they will not admit any good part to intermingle with them. But for which of my good parts did you first suffer love for me?

Benedick

Suffer love – a good epithet! I do suffer love indeed, for I love thee against my will.

Beatrice

In spite of your heart, I think; alas, poor heart! If you spite it for my sake, I will spite it for yours; for I will never love that which my friend hates.

Benedick

Thou and I are too wise to woo peaceably.

Beatrice

It appears not in this confession: there's not one wise man among twenty that will praise himself.

Benedick

An old, an old instance, Beatrice, that liv'd in the time of good neighbours; if a man do not erect in this age his own tomb ere he dies, he shall live no longer in monument than the bell rings and the widow weeps.

Beatrice

And how long is that, think you?

Benedick

Question: why, an hour in clamour, and a quarter in

78. ***rheum*** tears.
79. ***Don Worm*** the traditional 'worm of conscience' that eats away at you.

90–1. ***old coil*** total uproar.
93. ***abus'd*** deceived.
93. ***Don John is the author*** Don John is behind it.

rheum. Therefore is it most expedient for the wise, if Don Worm, his conscience, find no impediment to the contrary, to be the trumpet of his own virtues, as I am to myself. So much for praising myself, who, I myself will bear witness, is praiseworthy. And now tell me, how doth your cousin?

Beatrice

Very ill.

Benedick

And how do you?

Beatrice

Very ill too.

Benedick

Serve God, love me, and mend; there will I leave you too, for here comes one in haste.

[Enter URSULA.*]*

Ursula

Madam, you must come to your uncle. Yonder's old coil at home. It is proved my Lady Hero hath been falsely accus'd, the Prince and Claudio mightily abus'd; and Don John is the author of all, who is fled and gone. Will you come presently?

Beatrice

Will you go hear this news, signior?

Benedick

I will live in thy heart, die in thy lap, and be buried in thy eyes; and, more over, I will go with thee to thy uncle's.

[Exeunt.]

SCENE III

As Claudio and Don Pedro bring lighted-candles to Leonato's family monument, Claudio is shown as a humble young man, paying solemn respect to the young woman he harmed. This sombre scene acts as a counterpart to the one to come – which will reveal the truth in its totality, and bring renewed joy.

5. ***guerdon*** reward.

12. ***goddess of the night*** a reference to Diana, goddess of the moon and chastity.
13. ***slew*** killed.
13. ***knight*** follower, servant.

18. ***heavily*** mournfully, solemnly.

23. ***rite*** ceremony.

Scene III

A churchyard.

[Enter DON PEDRO, CLAUDIO, *and three or four with tapers.]*

Claudio

Is this the monument of Leonato?

A Lord

It is, my lord.

Claudio

[Reads from a scroll.]

Epitaph.
'Done to death by slanderous tongues
Was the Hero that here lies;
Death, in guerdon of her wrongs,
Gives her fame which never dies.
So the life that died with shame
Lives in death with glorious fame.'
Hang thou there upon the tomb,
Praising her when I am dumb.
Now, music, sound, and sing your solemn hymn.

Song.
Pardon, goddess of the night,
Those that slew thy virgin knight;
For the which, with songs of woe,
Round about her tomb they go.
Midnight, assist our moan;
Help us to sigh and groan,
Heavily, heavily.
Graves, yawn, and yield your dead,
Till death be uttered,
Heavily, heavily.

Claudio

Now, unto thy bones good night.
Yearly will I do this rite.

26. ***the wheels of Phoebus*** another name for Apollo, the sun god, who was believed to drive his chariot with the sun across the sky each morning.
27. ***Dapples*** speckles.
29. ***several*** separate.

30. ***weeds*** clothes.

32. ***Hymen*** god of marriage.
33. ***issue*** outcome.

Don Pedro
Good morrow, masters; put your torches out;
The wolves have prey'd; and look, the gentle day,
Before the wheels of Phoebus, round about
Dapples the drowsy east with spots of grey.
Thanks to you all, and leave us. Fare you well.

Claudio
Good morrow, masters; each his several way.

Don Pedro
Come, let us hence, and put on other weeds;
And then to Leonato's we will go.

Claudio
And Hymen now with luckier issue speed's
Than this for whom we rend'red up this woe.

[Exeunt.]

SCENE IV

Often in Shakespeare's plays, the final 'revelation' scene such as this one, untangles even larger and more complex webs but here the truth about Don John has already been revealed, and all that is left is for Hero to be unmasked. Although Benedick and Beatrice also discover the manner in which they were 'tricked' into loving each other, this revelation is light-hearted, and does not lead to their separation. The final news about Don John tells us that the villain has not got away with his crime, and will no doubt be punished.

5. ***against her will unintentionally*** (this may be rather kind to Margaret, and perhaps an indication that Shakespeare didn't want to open the 'problem' of how she should be dealt with).
6. ***question*** investigation.
7. ***sorts*** have turned out.

8. ***faith*** my vow to Beatrice.

14. ***office*** part.

17. ***confirm'd*** countenance straight face.

18. ***entreat your pains*** ask for your assistance.

20. ***undo*** ruin.

Scene IV

Leonato's house.

[Enter LEONATO, ANTONIO, BENEDICK, BEATRICE, MARGARET, URSULA, FRIAR FRANCIS, *and* HERO.*]*

Friar
Did I not tell you she was innocent?

Leonato
So are the Prince and Claudio, who accus'd her
Upon the error that you heard debated.
But Margaret was in some fault for this,
Although against her will, as it appears
In the true course of all the question.

Antonio
Well, I am glad that all things sorts so well.

Benedick
And so am I, being else by faith enforc'd
To call young Claudio to a reckoning for it.

Leonato
Well, daughter, and you gentlewomen all,
Withdraw into a chamber by yourselves;
And when I send for you, come hither mask'd.
The Prince and Claudio promis'd by this hour
To visit me. You know your office, brother:
You must be father to your brother's daughter,
And give her to young Claudio.

[Exeunt LADIES.*]*

Antonio
Which I will do with confirm'd countenance.

Benedick
Friar, I must entreat your pains, I think.

Friar
To do what, signior?

Benedick
To bind me, or undo me – one of them.

24. ***requite her*** return her love.

26. ***what's your will*** what do you want to do.

27. ***enigmatical*** puzzling, strange.

36. ***yet*** still.

38. ***Ethiope*** dark-skinned (pale skin was considered a sign of beauty in Elizabethan times).

Signior Leonato, truth it is, good signior,
Your niece regards me with an eye of favour.

Leonato
That eye my daughter lent her. 'Tis most true.

Benedick
And I do with an eye of love requite her.

Leonato
The sight whereof, I think, you had from me,
From Claudio, and the Prince. But what's your will?

Benedick
Your answer, sir, is enigmatical.
But, for my will, my will is your good will
May stand with ours, this day to be conjoin'd
In the state of honourable marriage;
In which, good friar, I shall desire your help.

Leonato
My heart is with your liking.

Friar
And my help.
Here comes the Prince and Claudio.

[Enter DON PEDRO *and* CLAUDIO, *with Attendants.]*

Don Pedro
Good morrow to this fair assembly.

Leonato
Good morrow, Prince; good morrow, Claudio;
We here attend you. Are you yet determin'd
To-day to marry with my brother's daughter?

Claudio
I'll hold my mind were she an Ethiope.

Leonato
Call her forth, brother; here's the friar ready.

[Exit ANTONIO.*]*

Don Pedro
Good morrow, Benedick.
Why, what's the matter

43. ***savage bull marriage*** (remember the reference to the 'savage bull's horns' in Act 5 Scene 1).
44. ***tip thy horns with gold*** make you look a fine cuckold.
45. ***all Europa*** all of Europe.
46. ***Europa did at lusty Jove*** The king of the gods, Jove, took on the form of a bull to carry off Europa, a beautiful princess.

50. ***got*** fathered.

52. ***For this I owe you*** I will pay you back for this.
52. ***reck'nings*** matters to be dealt with.

63. ***defil'd*** slandered.

That you have such a February face,
So full of frost, of storm, and cloudiness?

Claudio

I think he thinks upon the savage bull.
Tush, fear not, man; we'll tip thy horns with gold,
And all Europa shall rejoice at thee,
As once Europa did at lusty Jove,
When he would play the noble beast in love.

Benedick

Bull Jove, sir, had an amiable low;
And some such strange bull leap'd your father's cow,
And got a calf in that same noble feat
Much like to you, for you have just his bleat.

[Re-enter ANTONIO, *with the* LADIES *masked.]*

Claudio

For this I owe you. Here comes other reck'nings.
Which is the lady I must seize upon?

Antonio

This same is she, and I do give you her.

Claudio

Why, then she's mine. Sweet, let me see your face.

Leonato

No, that you shall not, till you take her hand
Before this friar, and swear to marry her.

Claudio

Give me your hand; before this holy friar
I am your husband, if you like of me.

Hero

And when I liv'd I was your other wife; *[Unmasking.]*
And when you lov'd you were my other husband.

Claudio

Another Hero!

Hero

Nothing certainer.
One Hero died defil'd; but I do live,
And, surely as I live, I am a maid.

66. ***but whiles*** only as long as.

67. ***qualify*** explain.

69. ***largely*** in full.
70. ***let wonder seem familiar*** let these surprises seem natural.

72. ***Soft and fair*** just a minute.

83. ***well-nigh*** almost (we might say 'practically...').

85. ***in friendly recompense*** in a friendly, joky way.

Don Pedro
The former Hero! Hero that is dead!
Leonato
She died, my lord, but whiles her slander liv'd.
Friar
All this amazement can I qualify,
When, after that the holy rites are ended,
I'll tell you largely of fair Hero's death.
Meantime let wonder seem familiar,
And to the chapel let us presently.
Benedick
Soft and fair, friar. Which is Beatrice?
Beatrice
I answer to that name. *[Unmasking]*
What is your will?
Benedick
Do not you love me?
Beatrice
Why no, no more than reason.
Benedick
Why, then your uncle, and the Prince, and Claudio,
Have been deceived: they swore you did.
Beatrice
Do not you love me?
Benedick
Troth no, no more than reason.
Beatrice
Why, then my cousin, Margaret, and Ursula,
Are much deceiv'd; for they did swear you did.
Benedick
They swore that you were almost sick for me.
Beatrice
They swore that you were well-nigh dead for me.
Benedick
'Tis no such matter. Then you do not love me?
Beatrice
No, truly, but in friendly recompense.

90. ***Fashioned*** inspired by, designed for.

91. ***hand*** handwriting.

98. ***in a consumption*** wasting away from a disease.

99. ***stop*** close up, block.

103. ***care for*** am afraid of.
103. ***epigram*** witty remark.

111. ***art like to be my kinsman*** are going to be related to me (because Hero and Beatrice are cousins).

Leonato

Come, cousin, I am sure you love the gentleman.

Claudio

And I'll be sworn upon't that he loves her;
For here's a paper written in his hand,
A halting sonnet of his own pure brain,
Fashion'd to Beatrice.

Hero

And here's another,
Writ in my cousin's hand, stol'n from her pocket,
Containing her affection unto Benedick.

Benedick

A miracle! here's our own hands against our hearts. Come, I will have thee; but, by this light, I take thee for pity.

Beatrice

I would not deny you; but, by this good day, I yield upon great persuasion; and partly to save your life, for I was told you were in a consumption.

Benedick

Peace; I will stop your mouth.

[Kissing her.]

Don Pedro

How dost thou. Benedick the married man?

Benedick

I'll tell thee what. Prince: a college of wit-crackers cannot flout me out of my humour. Dost thou think I care for a satire or an epigram? No. If a man will be beaten with brains, 'a shall wear nothing handsome about him. In brief, since I do purpose to marry, I will think nothing to any purpose that the world can say against it; and therefore never flout at me for what I have said against it; for man is a giddy thing, and this is my conclusion. For thy part, Claudio, I did think to have beaten thee; but in that thou art like to be my kinsman, live unbruis'd, and love my cousin.

114. ***cudgell'd*** beaten.

115. ***double dealer*** in the first sense, a deceiver – but then Claudio means it in the sense of a partner/companion as Benedick will also marry as he will.

116–7. ***do not look exceedingly narrowly to thee*** does not watch you closely.

124. ***staff*** walking stick.

125. ***ta'en in flight*** captured while on the run.

Claudio

I had well hop'd thou wouldst have denied Beatrice, that I might have cudgell'd thee out of thy single life, to make thee a double dealer; which out of question thou wilt be, if my cousin do not look exceeding narrowly to thee.

Benedick

Come, come, we are friends. Let's have a dance ere we are married, that we may lighten our own hearts and our wives' heels.

Leonato

We'll have dancing afterward.

Benedick

First, of my word; therefore play, music. Prince, thou art sad; get thee a wife, get thee a wife. There is no staff more reverend than one tipp'd with horn.

[Enter a MESSENGER.*]*

Messenger

My lord, your brother John is ta'en in flight,
And brought with armed men back to Messina.

Benedick

Think not on him till to-morrow.
I'll devise thee brave punishments for him.
Strike up, pipers.

[Dance. Exeunt.]

SUMMING UP

'Men were deceivers ever . . .' sings Balthasar in Act 2 Scene 3, but it is perhaps fair to say that with the exception of Don John, it is the men who learn most in the play. For Claudio, the experience of love, and his clumsy handling of its consequences, mean he undergoes a chastening journey, beginning as a noble young fighter, almost ending as a humbled man, forced to marry a girl he doesn't know. For Benedick, the confirmed bachelor, the experience of love, and having to submit to his lover's wishes (remember, he agrees to 'kill Claudio') makes him more complete. He is able to express love – and yet still joke – at his own wedding, 'though one wonders if he will ever really 'stop' Beatrice's mouth! Leonato experiences his own private hell, before emerging to see his daughter's reputation (and his) fully restored. It is never clear whether his sorrow is more for her, or for himself, but perhaps the two are so inextricably-linked that even he isn't clear about it. His speech at the first, ruined wedding, conveys how strongly what we are and what we mean is tied to our family and children . . .

I might have said 'No part of it is mine:
This shame derives itself from unknown loins'?
But mine, and mine I loved and mine I praised,
And mine that I was proud on – mine so much
That I myself was to myself not mine,
Valuing of her . . .

(Act 4 Scene 1)

The theme of family honour – and daughters' responsibility to fathers, runs through many Shakespeare plays (*Taming of the Shrew, Romeo and Juliet,* for example, to name a few) but nowhere is the consequence of shame and damaged love shown more graphically – some might say melodramatically – than here, especially as Leonato adds how Hero has 'fallen into a pit of ink . . .'

For the women of the play, they emerge rejuvenated and restored. Beatrice can be played by actresses almost sadly – as a joker who believes she will never find Mr Right and therefore gets her retaliations in first before she can be hurt. But this would be to deny audiences the delight in her vivid and (for its time) powerful commitment to woman's own independence of thought. She is not diminished by the trick played on her – after all, Benedick is equally deceived – and marriage is not a defeat, one hopes. It is partly her belief in Hero's innate goodness, and her ability to persuade Benedick to back the right horse (her) rather than the mistaken Don Pedro and Claudio, that saves the situation, even if it is the Friar's plan that provides the means to do it.

Hero is in one sense more of an enigma. Virtually invisible at the start of the play – a mere pawn in her father's plans – she emerges as a lively character in her own right as she organises the deception of Beatrice in Act 3 Scene 1. Some actresses have even identified a kind of cruelty in her words for Beatrice – a chance to dabble in the sorts of insults and mocking comments her cousin is known for, when she says . . .

'So turns she every man the wrong side out,
And never gives to truth and virtue that
Which simpleness and merit purchaseth . . .'

(Act 3 Scene 1)

One can almost imagine her sharpening her claws! But this too, would be unkind to Hero. Her own vulnerability in the face of Claudio's accusations is obvious, and she emerges in the final scene as a newly-made Hero, with her experience of the world's ability to inflict damage. She acknowledges that she is not the person she once was, even as she plays the part of her father's unwanted niece . . .

'And when I lived, I was your other wife;
And when you loved, you were my other husband . . .'

Claudio answers . . .

'Another Hero!'

. . . and indeed she is.

The play's punning title, *Much ado about Nothing* . . . which we now take to mean 'a lot of confusion and uproar over nothing very important', is rather misleading. What could be more important than choosing a husband and wife, the status of your reputation, your honour, and your family? Only the threat of death is missing – and even this is hinted at in the 'pretend' death of Hero. Don John's unrepentant villainy might cast a dark shadow over the play, too, but by the end he has been dispensed with – he doesn't appear after Act 4 Scene 1 – and it is just possible by the final wedding scene, to forget the unpleasantness that has gone before. This is largely due to Benedick and Beatrice, and it is appropriate that it is Benedick, rather than Claudio, Don Pedro or Leonato, to whom Shakespeare gives the final words – the command for the musicians to play, and for dance and laughter to be our abiding memories of Messina.

THEME INDEX

Deliberate Deception

In the play, the tricks and games played on people often have the best intentions – to make people fall in love; to help someone get what they want; to make someone realise their mistake. Not all, however, are well meant.

Act 2 Scene 1: The Ball: A masked Pedro woos Hero pretending to be Claudio (with his agreement); The masked Antonio tries to trick Ursula, but she recognises him; Benedick, also masked, tries to speak to Beatrice, but she knows it is him; Don John tells Claudio that Don Pedro intends to marry Hero.

Act 2 Scene 3: Benedick is tricked by Pedro, Leonato, and Claudio (with Balthasar present). Benedick thinks he is over-hearing their conversation. They know he is there!

Act 3 Scene 1: Hero and Ursula trick Beatrice. She thinks she is over-hearing their conversation. They know she is there.

Act 3 Scene 2: Don John tells Claudio and Pedro of Hero's sinful behaviour. They go off to see if it is true. The planned deception involves Borachio being seen with 'Hero' – actually Margaret, and it looking as if Hero is not as innocent as she seems.

Act 4 Scene 1: The first wedding Claudio turns up for the wedding and even goes through the early part of the ceremony, before refusing to accept Hero, as a result of her 'betrayal'. The Friar persuades Leonato to allow people to think that Hero is dead.

Act 5 Scene 4: the second wedding Claudio believes he is to marry a niece of Leonato's, but when Hero is unmasked, he realises she is alive and willingly takes her as his bride.

Love and marriage

It's easy to see why love and marriage as themes were so central to many of Shakespeare's play. Even more so than today, marriage was incredibly important. For a start, it was a financial arrangement between families, rarely just a 'love match'. Families needed to be sure their children married well. In addition, marriages make great drama – again, things can go wrong (as in *Much Ado*) but they can also be used for putting things right, and tying up the loose ends.

Act 1 Scene 1: Claudio falls for Hero; Benedick and Beatrice claim to dislike each other intensely.

Act 2 Scene 1: Marriage negotiations, and expressions of love, take place, in a variety of ways during the masked ball.

Act 2 Scene 3: Benedick is fooled into falling for Beatrice; he revises his opinion of marriage!

Act 3 Scene 1: Beatrice is similarly fooled into falling for Benedick, and we see a different side of her character.

Act 3 Scene 4: Hero's nervous preparations for marriage, and Beatrice's own lovesick behaviour focus almost exclusively on the effect of love and attraction.

Act 4 Scene 1: The twin themes of love and marriage are brought into sharp focus by Claudio's rejection of Hero, and point up the connection between marrying and honour. Benedick and Beatrice's own relationship – now more honest – provides a parallel to the youthful inexperience of Hero and Claudio.

Act 5 Scene 2: This short moving scene presents us with Benedick and Beatrice demonstrating and stating their love for each other, but also the responsibilities and expectations that come with it.

Act 5 Scene 4: the joint marriages of the two couples complete the play, and bring some form of honesty and equality to how each lover views his or her partner.

Family, honour and status

Act 1 Scene 1: Leonato is clearly proud to be welcoming the noble Don Pedro to his house and greets him with lively but appropriate behaviour and language.

Act 2 Scene 1: We are given a glimpse of the duties and responsibilities placed on women by the different ways in which Hero and Beatrice respond to the idea of marriage. On the one hand, Hero is compliant and willing to marry whoever her father deems suitable, whilst Beatrice says that even if it is important for her cousin to 'make curtsy' to her father, at least let the man she chooses be 'handsome'. Beatrice, the unattached, older woman can say this. Hero can't.

Act 2 Scene 3: Don John's sense of his own status and respect is challenged (in his own mind, at least) by Claudio. He feels rejected, and says he is 'sick in displeasure to him.'

Act 4 Scene 1: Claudio owes duty to Don Pedro, which is why when Hero appears to shame him, it is dishonouring Don Pedro, too. As Pedro says, *'I stand dishonoured that have gone about/To link my dear friend to a common stale.'*

Leonato feels equally shamed by his daughter's behaviour, saying *'. . . she is fallen/Into a pit of ink . . .'*

Act 5 Scene 1: Equally, when she is proved innocent he seeks revenge on the men who wronged her. So, too, does Antonio. The family honour has been attacked. *God knows, I loved my niece,/And she is dead, slandered to death by villains . . .*

The penance that Claudio and Pedro do, once they discover Hero is innocent, is not just to pray at her 'monument', but, more importantly, to . . . *possess the people in Messina here,/How innocent she died* . . . This is to ensure the people know Hero (and Hero's family) are innocent of any crime or shameful act.

Act 5 Scene 4: The final marriage is as much about Hero's rebirth as a newly-respected woman, an equal to Claudio, not his ignorant, romanticised fantasy. Her honour and status has been regained.

Self-deception

Most of the deceptions in the play are caused by others, but people are also deceived about themselves. This means they fail to see the truth about their own characters, or what is happening to them.

Beatrice: On the surface Beatrice appears to have no interest in pursuing a man or getting married. *'I had rather hear my dog bark at a crow than a man swear he loves me . . .'* she says in Act 1 Scene 1. However, by Act 3 Scene 1 she is prepared to accept that her previous attitude created an image she was no altogether pleased with. As she says, *'Stand I condemned for pride and scorn so much? . . .'*

Benedick: he is also deceiving himself when he says, *'It is certain I am loved of all ladies, only you excepted . . .'* to Beatrice in the first scene of the play, and also vows that he will *'. . . live a bachelor . . .'* and proceeds to make fun of the love-sick Claudio, little realising what the future holds for him. In reality, as soon as he believes he is loved by Beatrice, he alters what he said only a short while before . . .*When I said I would die a bachelor, I did not think I should live till I were married . . .* (Act 2 Scene 3).

Claudio: he is under the illusion that love is a simple and clear matter – and that the world is for laughter and love. But Don John's plotting – and his own willingness to believe the worst of Hero in Act 4 Scene 1 – makes him grow up very quickly.

Hero: Hero's self-deception occurs because she believes the world to be a simple place in which people's words and actions can be trusted. She has never faced villainy such as that practised by Don John and has been protected in her little world of Messina. She is damaged by the outer world – is changed forever.

Don Pedro: he fools himself by believing he can exert complete power over the world around him. He suggests and sets up in Act 2 Scene 1 the love affair between Benedick and Beatrice, and helps arrange Hero and

Claudio's marriage – but even he cannot control his the evil intentions of Don John.

Leonato: he deceives himself, initially, by thinking that his own daughter could be capable of shameful behaviour when confronted by Claudio in Act 4 Scene 1. In many ways, his self-deception is the most extreme of all – to believe his own daughter capable of betrayal the night before her wedding. It takes the combined efforts of The Friar, Benedick and Beatrice, to make him see sense.

Shakespeare: Words and Phrases

adapted from the Collins English Dictionary

abate 1 VERB to abate here means to lessen or diminish ❑ *There lives within the very flame of love/ A kind of wick or snuff that will abate it* (*Hamlet 4.7*) 2 VERB to abate here means to shorten ❑ *Abate thy hours* (*A Midsummer Night's Dream 3.2*) 3 VERB to abate here means to deprive ❑ *She hath abated me of half my train* (*King Lear 2.4*)

abjure VERB to abjure means to renounce or give up ❑ *this rough magic I here abjure* (*Tempest 5.1*)

abroad ADV abroad means elsewhere or everywhere ❑ *You have heard of the news abroad* (*King Lear 2.1*)

abrogate VERB to abrogate means to put an end to ❑ *so it shall praise you to abrogate scurrility* (*Love's Labours Lost 4.2*)

abuse 1 NOUN abuse in this context means deception or fraud ❑ *What should this mean? Are all the rest come back?/ Or is it some abuse, and no such thing?* (*Hamlet 4.7*) 2 NOUN an abuse in this context means insult or offence ❑ *I will be deaf to pleading and excuses/ Nor tears nor prayers shall purchase our abuses* (*Romeo and Juliet 3.1*) 3 NOUN an abuse in this context means using something improperly ❑ *we'll digest/ Th'abuse of distance* (*Henry II Chorus*) 4 NOUN an abuse in this context means doing something which is corrupt or dishonest ❑ *Come, bring them away: if these be good people in a commonweal that do nothing but their abuses in common houses, I know no law: bring them away.* (*Measure for Measure 2.1*)

abuser NOUN the abuser here is someone who betrays, a betrayer ❑ *I ... do attach thee/ For an abuser of the world* (*Othello 1.2*)

accent NOUN accent here means language ❑ *In states unborn, and accents yet unknown* (*Julius Caesar 3.1*)

accident NOUN an accident in this context is an event or something that happened ❑ *think no more of this night's accidents* (*A Midsummer Night's Dream 4.1*)

accommodate VERB to accommodate in this context means to equip or to give someone the equipment to do something ❑ *The safer sense will ne'er accommodate/ His master thus.* (*King Lear 4.6*)

according ADJ according means sympathetic or ready to agree ❑ *within the scope of choice/ Lies* *my consent and fair according voice* (*Romeo and Juliet 1.2*)

account NOUN account often means judgement (by God) or reckoning ❑ *No reckoning made, but sent to my account/ With all my imperfections on my head* (*Hamlet 1.5*)

accountant ADJ accountant here means answerable or accountable ❑ *his offence is... /Accountant to the law* (*Measure for Measure 2.4*)

ace NOUN ace here means one or first referring to the lowest score on a dice ❑ *No die, but an ace, for him; for he is but one./ Less than an ace, man; for he is dead; he is nothing.* (*A Midsummer Night's Dream 5.1*)

acquit VERB here acquit means to be rid of or free of. It is related to the verb quit ❑ *I am glad I am so acquit of this tinderbox* (*The Merry Wives of Windsor 1.3*)

afeard ADJ afeard means afraid or frightened ❑ *Nothing afeard of what thyself didst make* (*Macbeth 1.3*)

affiance NOUN affiance means confidence or trust ❑ *O how hast thou with jealousy infected/ The sweetness of affiance* (*Henry V 2.2*)

affinity NOUN in this context, affinity means important connections, or relationships with important people ❑ *The Moor replies/ That he you hurt is of great fame in Cyprus,/ And great affinity* (*Othello 3.1*)

agnize VERB to agnize is an old word that means that you recognize or acknowledge something ❑ *I do agnize/ A natural and prompt alacrity I find in hardness* (*Othello 1.3*)

ague NOUN an ague is a fever in which the patient has hot and cold shivers one after the other ❑ *This is some monster of the isle with four legs, who hath got ... an ague* (*The Tempest 2.2*)

alarm, alarum NOUN an alarm or alarum is a call to arms or a signal for soldiers to prepare to fight ❑ *Whence cometh this alarum and the noise?* (*Henry VI part I 1.4*)

Albion NOUN Albion is another word for England ❑ *but I will sell my dukedom,/ To buy a slobbery and a dirty farm In that nook-shotten isle of Albion* (*Henry V 3.5*)

all of all PHRASE all of all means everything, or the sum of all things ❑ *The very all of all* (*Love's Labours Lost 5.1*)

amend VERB amend in this context means to get better or to heal ❑ *at his touch... They presently amend* (*Macbeth 4.3*)

anchor VERB if you anchor on something you concentrate on it or fix on it ❑ *My invention ... Anchors on Isabel* (*Measure for Measure 2.4*)

anon ADV anon was a common word for soon ❑ *You shall see anon how the murderer gets the love of Gonzago's wife* (*Hamlet 3.2*)

antic 1 ADJ antic here means weird or strange ❑ *I'll charm the air to give a sound/ While you perform your antic round* (*Macbeth 4.1*) 2 NOUN in this context antic means a clown or a strange, unattractive creature ❑ *If black, why nature, drawing an antic,/ Made a foul blot* (*Much Ado About Nothing 3.1*)

apace ADV apace was a common word for quickly ❑ *Come apace* (*As You Like It 3.3*)

apparel NOUN apparel means clothes or clothing ❑ *one suit of apparel* (*Hamlet 3.2*)

appliance NOUN appliance here means cure ❑ *Diseases desperate grown/ By desperate appliance are relieved* (*Hamlet 4.3*)

argument NOUN argument here means a topic of conversation or the subject ❑ *Why 'tis the rarest argument of wonder that hath shot out in our latter times* (*All's Well That Ends Well 2.3*)

arrant ADJ arrant means absolute, complete. It strengthens the meaning of a noun ❑ *Fortune, that arrant whore* (*King Lear 2.4*)

arras NOUN an arras is a tapestry, a large cloth with a picture sewn on it using coloured thread ❑ *Behind the arras I'll convey myself/ To hear the process* (*Hamlet 3.3*)

art 1 NOUN art in this context means knowledge ❑ *Their malady convinces/ The great essay of art* (*Macbeth 4.3*) 2 NOUN art can also mean skill as it does here ❑ *He ... gave you such a masterly report/ For art and exercise in your defence* (*Hamlet 4.7*) 3 NOUN art here means magic ❑ *Now I want/ Spirits to enforce, art to enchant* (*The Tempest 5 Epilogue*)

assay 1 NOUN an assay was an attempt, a try ❑ *Make assay./ Bow, stubborn knees* (*Hamlet 3.3*) 2 NOUN assay can also mean a test or a trial ❑ *he hath made assay of her virtue* (*Measure for Measure 3.1*)

attend (on/upon) VERB attend on means to wait for or to expect ❑ *Tarry I here, I but attend on death* (*Two Gentlemen of Verona 3.1*)

auditor NOUN an auditor was a member of an audience or someone who listens ❑ *I'll be an auditor* (*A Midsummer Night's Dream 3.1*)

aught NOUN aught was a common word which meant anything ❑ *if my love thou holdest at aught* (*Hamlet 4.3*)

aunt 1 NOUN an aunt was another word for an old woman and also means someone who talks a lot or a gossip ❑ *The wisest aunt telling the saddest tale* (*A Midsummer Night's Dream 2.1*) 2 NOUN aunt could also mean a mistress or a prostitute ❑ *the thrush and the jay/ Are summer songs for me and my aunts/ While we lie tumbling in the hay* (*The Winter's Tale 4.3*)

avaunt EXCLAM avaunt was a common word which meant go away ❑ *Avaunt, you curs!* (*King Lear 3.6*)

aye ADV here aye means always or ever ❑ *Whose state and honour I for aye allow* (*Richard II 5.2*)

baffle VERB baffle meant to be disgraced in public or humiliated ❑ *I am disgraced, impeached, and baffled here* (*Richard II 1.1*)

bald ADJ bald means trivial or silly ❑ *I knew 'twould be a bald conclusion* (*The Comedy of Errors 2.2*)

ban NOUN a ban was a curse or an evil spell ❑ *Sometimes with lunatic bans... Enforce their charity* (*King Lear 2.3*)

barren ADJ barren meant empty or hollow ❑ *now I let go your hand, I am barren.* (*Twelfth Night 1.3*)

base ADJ base is an adjective that means unworthy or dishonourable ❑ *civet is of a baser birth than tar* (*As You Like It 3.2*)

base 1 ADJ base can also mean of low social standing or someone who was not part of the ruling class ❑ *Why brand they us with 'base'?* (*King Lear 1.2*) 2 ADJ here base means poor quality ❑ *Base cousin,/ Darest thou break first?* (*Two Noble Kinsmen 3.3*)

bawdy NOUN bawdy means obscene or rude ❑ *Bloody, bawdy villain!* (*Hamlet 2.2*)

bear in hand PHRASE bear in hand means taken advantage of or fooled ❑ *This I made good to you In our last conference, passed in probation with you/ How you were borne in hand* (*Macbeth 3.1*)

beard VERB to beard someone was to oppose or confront them ❑ *Com'st thou to beard me in Denmark?* (*Hamlet 2.2*)

beard, in one's PHRASE if you say something in someone's beard you say it to their face ❑ *I will verify as much in his beard* (*Henry V 3.2*)

beaver NOUN a beaver was a visor on a battle helmet ❑ *O yes, my lord, he wore his beaver up* (*Hamlet 1.2*)

become VERB if something becomes you it suits you or is appropriate to you ❑ *Nothing in his life became him like the leaving it* (*Macbeth 1.4*)

bed, brought to PHRASE to be brought to bed means to give birth ❑ *His wife but yesternight was brought to bed* (*Titus Andronicus 4.2*)

bedabbled ADJ if something is bedabbled it is sprinkled ❑ *Bedabbled with the dew, and torn with briers* (*A Midsummer Night's Dream 3.2*)

Bedlam NOUN Bedlam was a word used for Bethlehem Hospital which was a place the insane were sent to ❑ *The country give me proof and precedent/ Of Bedlam beggars* (*King Lear 2.3*)

bed-swerver NOUN a bed-swerver was someone who was unfaithful in marriage, an adulterer ❑ *she's/ A bed-swerver* (*Winter's Tale 2.1*)

befall 1 VERB to befall is to happen, occur or take place ❑ *In this same interlude it doth befall/ That I present a wall* (*A Midsummer Night's Dream 5.1*) 2 VERB to befall can also mean to happen to someone or something ❑ *fair befall thee and thy noble house* (*Richard III 1.3*)

behoof NOUN behoof was an advantage or benefit ❑ *All our surgeons/ Convent in their behoof* (*Two Noble Kinsmen 1.4*)

beldam NOUN a beldam was a witch or old woman ❑ *Have I not reason, beldams as you are?* (*Macbeth 3.5*)

belike ADV belike meant probably, perhaps or presumably ❑ *belike he likes it not* (*Hamlet 3.2*)

bent 1 NOUN bent means a preference or a direction ❑ *Let me work,/ For I can give his humour true bent,/ And I will bring him to the Capitol* (*Julius Caesar 2.1*) 2 ADJ if you are bent on something you are determined to do it ❑ *for now I am bent to know/ By the worst means the worst.* (*Macbeth 3.4*)

beshrew VERB beshrew meant to curse or wish evil on someone ❑ *much beshrew my manners and my pride/ If Hermia meant to say Lysander lied* (*A Midsummer Night's Dream 2.2*)

betime (s) ADV betime means early ❑ *To business that we love we rise betime* (*Antony and Cleopatra 4.4*)

bevy NOUN bevy meant type or sort, it was also used to mean company ❑ *many more of the same bevy* (*Hamlet 5.2*)

blazon VERB to blazon something meant to display or show it ❑ *that thy skill be more to blazon it* (*Romeo and Juliet 2.6*)

blind ADJ if you are blind when you do something you are reckless or do not care about the consequences ❑ *are you yet to your own souls so blind/ That two you will war with God by murdering me* (*Richard III 1.4*)

bombast NOUN bombast was wool stuffing (used in a cushion for example) and so it came to mean padded out or long-winded. Here it means someone who talks a lot about nothing in particular ❑ *How now my sweet creature of bombast* (*Henry IV part I 2.4*)

bond 1 NOUN a bond is a contract or legal deed ❑ *Well, then, your bond, and let me see* (*Merchant of Venice 1.3*) 2 NOUN bond could also mean duty or commitment ❑ *I love your majesty/ According to my bond* (*King Lear 1.1*)

bottom NOUN here bottom means essence, main point or intent ❑ *Now I see/ The bottom of your purpose* (*All's Well That Ends Well 3.7*)

bounteously ADV bounteously means plentifully, abundantly ❑ *I prithee, and I'll pay thee bounteously* (*Twelfth Night 1.2*)

brace 1 NOUN a brace is a couple or two ❑ *Have lost a brace of kinsmen* (*Romeo and Juliet 5.3*) 2 NOUN if you are in a brace position it means you are ready ❑ *For that it stands not in such warlike brace* (*Othello 1.3*)

brand VERB to mark permanantly like the markings on cattle ❑ *the wheeled seat/ Of fortunate Caesar ... branded his baseness that ensued* (*Anthony and Cleopatra 4.14*)

brave ADJ brave meant fine, excellent or splendid ❑ *O brave new world/ That has such people in't* (*The Tempest 5.1*)

brine NOUN brine is sea-water ❑ *He shall drink nought brine, for I'll not show him/ Where the quick freshes are* (*The Tempest 3.2*)

brow NOUN brow in this context means appearance ❑ *doth hourly grow/ Out of his brows* (*Hamlet 3.3*)

burden 1 NOUN the burden here is a chorus ❑ *I would sing my song without a burden* (*As You Like It 3.2*) 2 NOUN burden means load or weight (this is the current meaning) ❑ *the scarfs and the bannerets about thee did manifoldly dissuade me from believing thee a vessel of too great a burden* (*All's Well that Ends Well 2.3*)

buttons, in one's PHRASE this is a phrase that means clear, easy to see ❑ *Tis in his buttons he will carry't* (*The Merry Wives of Windsor 3.2*)

cable NOUN cable here means scope or reach ❑ *The law ... Will give her cable* (*Othello 1.2*)

cadent ADJ if something is cadent it is falling or dropping ❑ *With cadent tears fret channels in her cheeks* (*King Lear 1.4*).

canker VERB to canker is to decay, become corrupt ❑ *And, as with age his body uglier grows,/ So his mind cankers* (*The Tempest 4.1*)

canon, from the PHRASE from the canon is an expression meaning out of order, improper ❑ *Twas from the canon* (*Coriolanus 3.1*)

cap-a-pie ADV cap-a-pie means from head to foot, completely ❑ *I am courtier cap-a-pie* (*The Winter's Tale 4.4*)

carbonadoed ADJ if something is carbonadoed it is cut or scored (scratched) with a knife ❑ *it is your carbonadoed* (*All's Well That Ends Well 4.5*)

carouse VERB to carouse is to drink at length, party ❑ *They cast their caps up and carouse together* (*Anthony and Cleopatra 4.12*)

carrack NOUN a carrack was a large old ship, a galleon ❑ *Faith, he tonight hath boarded a land-carrack* (*Othello 1.2*)

cassock NOUN a cassock here means a military cloak, long coat ❑ *half of the which dare not shake the snow from off their cassocks lest they shake themselves to pieces* (*All's Well That Ends Well 4.3*)

catastrophe NOUN catastrophe here means conclusion or end ❑ *pat he comes, like the catastrophe of the old comedy* (*King Lear 1.2*)

cautel NOUN a cautel was a trick or a deceptive act ❑ *Perhaps he loves you now/ And now no soil not cautel doth besmirch* (*Hamlet 1.2*)

celerity NOUN celerity was a common word for speed, swiftness ❑ *Hence hath offence his quick celerity/ When it is borne in high authority* (*Measure for Measure 4.2*)

chafe NOUN chafe meant anger or temper ❑ *this Herculean Roman does become/ The carriage of his chafe* (*Anthony and Cleopatra 1.3*)

chanson NOUN chanson was an old word for a song ❑ *The first row of the pious chanson will show you more* (*Hamlet 2.2*)

chapman NOUN a chapman was a trader or merchant ❑ *Not uttered by base sale of chapman's tongues* (*Love's Labours Lost 2.1*)

chaps, chops NOUN chaps (and chops) was a word for jaws ❑ *Which ne'er shook hands nor bade farewell to him/ Till he unseamed him from the nave to th' chops* (*Macbeth 1.2*)

chattels NOUN chattels were your moveable possessions. The word is used in the traditional marriage ceremony ❑ *She is my goods, my chattels* (*The Taming of the Shrew 3.3*)

chide VERB if you are chided by someone you are told off or reprimanded ❑ *Now I but chide, but I should use thee worse* (*A Midsummer Night's Dream 3.2*)

chinks NOUN chinks was a word for cash or money ❑ *he that can lay hold of her/ Shall have the chinks* (*Romeo and Juliet 1.5*)

choleric ADJ if something was called choleric it meant that they were quick to get angry ❑ *therewithal unruly waywardness that infirm and choleric years bring with them* (*King Lear 1.1*)

chuff NOUN a chuff was a miser,

someone who clings to his or her money ❑ *ye fat chuffs* (*Henry IV part I* 2.2)

cipher NOUN cipher here means nothing ❑ *Mine were the very cipher of a function* (*Measure for Measure* 2.2)

circummured ADJ circummured means that something is surrounded with a wall ❑ *He hath a garden circummured with brick* (*Measure for Measure* 4.1)

civet NOUN a civet is a type of scent or perfume ❑ *Give me an ounce of civet* (*King Lear* 4.6)

clamorous ADJ clamorous means noisy or boisterous ❑ *Be clamorous and leap all civil bounds* (*Twelfth Night* 1.4)

clangour, clangor NOUN clangour is a word that means ringing (the sound that bells make) ❑ *Like to a dismal clangour heard from far* (*Henry VI part III* 2.3)

cleave VERB if you cleave to something you stick to it or are faithful to it ❑ *Thy thoughts I cleave to* (*The Tempest* 4.1)

clock and clock, 'twixt PHRASE from hour to hour, without stopping or continuously ❑ *To weep 'twixt clock and clock* (*Cymbeline* 3.4)

close ADJ here close means hidden ❑ *Stand close; this is the same Athenian* (*A Midsummer Night's Dream* 3.2)

cloud NOUN a cloud on your face means that you have a troubled, unhappy expression ❑ *He has cloud in's face* (*Anthony and Cleopatra* 3.2)

cloy VERB if you cloy an appetite you satisfy it ❑ *Other women cloy/The appetites they feed* (*Anthony and Cleopatra* 2.2)

cock-a-hoop, set PHRASE if you set cock-a-hoop you become free of everything ❑ *You will set cock-a-hoop* (*Romeo and Juliet* 1.5)

colours NOUN colours is a word used to describe battle-flags or banners. Sometimes we still say that we nail our colours to the mast if we are stating which team or side of an argument we support ❑ *the approbation of those that weep this lamentable divorce under her colours* (*Cymbeline* 1.5)

combustion NOUN combustion was a word meaning disorder or chaos ❑ *prophesying ... Of dire combustion and confused events* (*Macbeth* 2.3)

comely ADJ if you are or something is comely you or it is lovely, beautiful, graceful ❑ *O, what a world is this, when what is comely/Envenoms him that bears it!* (*As You Like It* 2.3)

commend VERB if you commend yourself to someone you send greetings to them ❑ *Commend me to my brother* (*Measure for Measure* 1.4)

compact NOUN a compact is an agreement or a contract ❑ *what compact mean you to have with us?* (*Julius Caesar* 3.1)

compass 1 NOUN here compass means range or scope ❑ *you would sound me from my lowest note to the top of my compass* (*Hamlet* 3.2) 2 VERB to compass here means to achieve, bring about or make happen ❑ *How now shall this be compassed?/Canst thou bring me to the party?* (*Tempest* 3.2)

comptible ADJ comptible is an old word meaning sensitive ❑ *I am very comptible, even to the least sinister usage.* (*Twelfth Night 1.5*)

confederacy NOUN a confederacy is a group of people usually joined together to commit a crime. It is another word for a conspiracy ❑ *Lo, she is one of this confederacy!* (*A Midsummer Night's Dream 3.2*)

confound VERB if you confound something you confuse it or mix it up; it also means to stop or prevent ❑ *A million fail, confounding oath on oath.* (*A Midsummer Night's Dream 3.2*)

contagion NOUN contagion is an old word for disease or poison ❑ *hell itself breathes out/ Contagion to this world* (*Hamlet 3.2*)

contumely NOUN contumely is an old word for an insult ❑ *the proud man's contumely* (*Hamlet 3.1*)

counterfeit 1 VERB if you counterfeit something you copy or imitate it ❑ *Meantime your cheeks do counterfeit our roses* (*Henry VI part I 2.4*) 2 VERB in this context counterfeit means to pretend or make believe ❑ *I will counterfeit the bewitchment of some popular man* (*Coriolanus*)

coz NOUN coz was a shortened form of the word cousin ❑ *sweet my coz, be merry* (*As You Like It 1.2*)

cozenage NOUN cozenage is an old word meaning cheating or a deception ❑ *Thrown out his angle for my proper life,/ And with such coz'nage* (*Hamlet 5.2*)

crave VERB crave used to mean to beg or request ❑ *I crave your pardon* (*The Comedy of Errors 1.2*)

crotchet NOUN crotchets are strange ideas or whims ❑ *thou hast some strange crotchets in thy head now* (*The Merry Wives of Windsor 2.1*)

cuckold NOUN a cuckold is a man whose wife has been unfaithful to him ❑ *As there is no true cuckold but calamity* (*Twelfth Night 1.5*)

cuffs, go to PHRASE this phrase meant to fight ❑ *the player went to cuffs in the question* (*Hamlet 2.2*)

cup VERB in this context cup is a verb which means to pour drink or fill glasses with alcohol ❑ *cup us til the world go round* (*Anthony and Cleopatra 2.7*)

cur NOUN cur is an insult meaning dog and is also used to mean coward ❑ *Out, dog! out, cur! Thou drivest me past the bounds/ Of maiden's patience* (*A Midsummer Night's Dream 3.2*)

curiously ADV in this context curiously means carefully or skilfully ❑ *The sleeves curiously cut* (*The Taming of the Shrew 4.3*)

curry VERB curry means to flatter or to praise someone more than they are worth ❑ *I would curry with Master Shallow that no man could better command his servants* (*Henry IV part II 5.1*)

custom NOUN custom is a habit or a usual practice ❑ *Hath not old custom made this life more sweet/ Than that of painted pomp?* (*As You Like It 2.1*)

cutpurse NOUN a cutpurse is an old word for a thief. Men used to carry their money in small bags (purse) that hung from their belts; thieves would cut the purse from the belt and steal their money ❑ *A cutpurse of the empire and the rule* (*Hamlet 3.4*)

dainty ADJ dainty used to mean splendid, fine ❑ *Why, that's my dainty Ariel!* (*Tempest 5.1*)

dally VERB if you dally with something you play with it or tease it ❑ *They that dally nicely with words may quickly make them wanton* (*Twelfth Night 3.1*)

damask COLOUR damask is a light-red or pink colour ❑ *Twas just the difference/ Betwixt the constant red and mingled damask* (*As You Like It 3.5*)

dare 1 VERB dare means to challeng or, confront ❑ *He goes before me, and still dares me on* (*A Midsummer Night's Dream 3.3*) 2 VERB dare in this context means to present, deliver or inflict ❑ *all that fortune, death, and danger dare* (*Hamlet 4.4*)

darkly ADV darkly was used in this context to mean secretly or cunningly ❑ *I will go darkly to work with her* (*Measure for Measure 5.1*)

daw NOUN a daw was a slang term for idiot or fool (after the bird jackdaw which was famous for its stupidity) ❑ *Yea, just so much as you may take upon a knife's point and choke a daw withal* (*Much Ado About Nothing 3.1*)

debile ADJ debile meant weak or feeble ❑ *And debile minister great power* (*All's Well That Ends Well 2.3*)

deboshed ADJ deboshed was another way of saying corrupted or debauched ❑ *Men so disordered, deboshed and bold* (*King Lear 1.4*)

decoct VERB to decoct was to heat up, warm something ❑ *Can sodden water,/ A drench for sur-reained jades ... Decoct their cold blood to such valiant heat?* (*Henry V 3.5*)

deep-revolving ADJ deep-revolving here uses the idea that you turn something over in your mind when you are thinking hard about it and so means deep-thinking, meditating ❑ *The deep-revolving Buckingham/ No more shall be the neighbour to my counsels* (*Richard III 4.2*)

defect NOUN defect here means shortcoming or something that is not right ❑ *Being unprepared/ Our will became the servant to defect* (*Macbeth 2.1*)

degree 1 NOUN degree here means rank, standing or station ❑ *Should a like language use to all degrees,/ And mannerly distinguishment leave out/ Betwixt the prince and beggar* (*The Winter's Tale 2.1*) 2 NOUN in this context, degree means extent or measure ❑ *her offence/ Must be of such unnatural degree* (*King Lear 1.1*)

deify VERB if you deify something or someone you worship it or them as a God ❑ *all.. deifying the name of Rosalind* (*As You Like It 3.2*)

delated ADJ delated here means detailed ❑ *the scope/ Of these delated articles* (*Hamlet 1.2*)

delicate ADJ if something was described as delicate it meant it was of fine quality or valuable ❑ *thou wast a spirit too delicate* (*The Tempest 1.2*)

demise VERB in this context demise means to transmit, give or convey ❑ *what state ... Canst thou demise to any child of mine?* (*Richard III 4.4*)

deplore VERB to deplore means to express with grief or sorrow ❑ *Never more/ Will I my master's tears to you deplore* (*Twelfth Night 3.1*)

depose VERB if you depose someone you make them take an oath, or swear something to be true ❑ *Depose him in the justice of his cause* (*Richard II 1.3*)

depositary NOUN a depositary is a trustee ❑ *Made you ... my depositary* (*King Lear 2.4*)

derive 1 VERB to derive means to comes from or to descend (it usually applies to people) ❑ *No part of it is mine,/ This shame derives itself from unknown loins.* (*Much Ado About Nothing 4.1*) 2 VERB if you derive something from someone you inherit it ❑ *Treason is not inherited ...Or, if we derive it from our friends/ What's that to me?* (*As You Like It 1.3*)

descry VERB to see or catch sight of ❑ *The news is true, my lord. He is descried* (*Anthony and Cleopatra 3.7*)

desert 1 NOUN desert means worth or merit ❑ *That dost in vile misproson shackle up/ My love and her desert* (*All's Well That Ends Well 2.3*) 2 ADJ desert is used here to mean lonely or isolated ❑ *if that love or gold/ Can in this desert place buy entertainment* (*As You LIke It 2.4*)

design 1 VERB to design means to indicate or point out ❑ *we shall see/ Justice design the victor's chivalry* (*Richard II 1.1*) 2 NOUN a design is a plan, an intention or an undertaking ❑ *hinder not the honour of his design* (*All's Well That Ends Well 3.6*)

designment NOUN a designment was a plan or undertaking ❑ *The desperate tempest hath so bang'd the Turks,/ That their designment halts* (*Othello 2.1*)

despite VERB despite here means to spite or attempt to thwart a plan ❑ *Only to despite them I will endeavour anything* (*Much Ado About Nothing 2.2*)

device NOUN a device is a plan, plot or trick ❑ *Excellent, I smell a device* (*Twelfth Night 2.3*)

disable VERB to disable here means to devalue or make little of ❑ *he disabled my judgement* (*As You Like It 5.4*)

discandy VERB here discandy means to melt away or dissolve ❑ *The hearts ... do discandy , melt their sweets* (*Anthony and Cleopatra 4.12*)

disciple VERB to disciple is to teach or train ❑ *He ...was/ Discipled of the bravest* (*All's Well That Ends Well 1.2*)

discommend VERB if you discommend something you criticize it ❑ *my dialect which you discommend so much* (*King Lear 2.2*)

discourse NOUN discourse means conversation, talk or chat ❑ *which part of it I'll waste/ With such discourse as I not doubt shall make it/ Go quick away* (*The Tempest 5.1*)

discover VERB discover used to mean to reveal or show ❑ *the Prince discovered to Claudio that he loved my niece* (*Much Ado About Nothing 1.2*)

disliken VERB disguise, make unlike ❑ *disliken/ The truth of your own seeming* (*The Winter's Tale 4.4*)

dismantle VERB to dismantle is to remove or take away ❑ *Commit a thing so monstrous to dismantle/*

So many folds of favour (*King Lear 1.1*)

disponge VERB dispongee means to pour out or rain down ❑ *The poisonous damp of night disponge upon me* (*Anthony and Cleopatra 4.9*)

distrain VERB to distrain something is to confiscate it ❑ *My father's goods are all distrained and sold* (*Richard II 2.3*)

divers ADJ divers is an old word for various ❑ *I will give out divers schedules of my beauty* (*Twelfth Night 1.5*)

doff VERB to doff is to get rid of or dispose ❑ *make our women fight/ To doff their dire distresses* (*Macbeth 4.3*)

dog VERB if you dog someone or something you follow them or it closely ❑ *I will rather leave to see Hector than not to dog him* (*Troilus and Cressida 5.1*)

dotage NOUN dotage here means infatuation ❑ *Her dotage now I do begin to pity* (*A Midsummer NIght's Dream 4.1*)

dotard NOUN a dotard was an old fool ❑ *I speak not like a dotard nor a fool* (*Much Ado About Nothing 5.1*)

dote VERB to dote is to love, cherish, care without seeing any fault ❑ *And won her soul; and she, sweet lady, dotes,/ Devoutly dotes, dotes in idolatry* (*A Midsummer Night's Dream 1.1*)

doublet NOUN a doublet was a man's close-fitting jacket with short skirt ❑ *Lord Hamlet, with his doublet all unbraced* (*Hamlet 2.1*)

dowager NOUN a dowager is a widow ❑ *Like to a step-dame or a dowage* (*A Midsummer Night's Dream 1.1*)

dowdy NOUN a dowdy was an ugly woman ❑ *Dido was a dowdy* (*Romeo and Juliet 2.4*)

dower NOUN a dower (or dowery) is the riches or property given by the father of a bride to her husband-to-be ❑ *Thy truth then by they dower* (*King Lear 1.1*)

dram NOUN a dram is a tiny amount ❑ *Why, everything adheres together that no dram of a scruple* (*Twelfth Night 3.4*)

drift NOUN drift is a plan, scheme or intention ❑ *Shall Romeo by my letters know our drift* (*Romeo and Juliet 4.1*)

dropsied ADJ dropsied means pretentious ❑ *Where great additions swell's and virtues none/ It is a dropsied honour* (*All's Well That Ends Well 2.3*)

drudge NOUN a drudge was a slave, servant ❑ *If I be his cuckold, he's my drudge* (*All's Well That Ends Well 1.3*)

dwell VERB to dwell sometimes meant to exist, to be ❑ *I'd rather dwell in my necessity* (*Merchant of Venice 1.3*)

earnest ADJ an earnest was a pledge to pay or a payment in advance ❑ *for an earnest of a greater honour/ He bade me from him call thee Thane of Cawdor* (*Macbeth 1.3*)

ecstasy NOUN madness ❑ *This is the very ecstasy of love* (*Hamlet 2.1*)

edict NOUN law or declaration ❑ *It stands as an edict in destiny.* (*A Midsummer Night's Dream 1.1*)

egall ADJ egall is an old word meaning equal ❑ *companions/ Whose souls do bear an egall yoke of love* (*Merchant of Venice 2.4*)

eisel NOUN eisel meant vinegar ❑ *Woo't drink up eisel?* (*Hamlet 5.1*)

eke, eke out VERB eke meant to add to, to increase. Eke out nowadays means to make something last as long as possible – particularly in the sense of making money last a long time ❑ *Still be kind/ And eke out our performance with your mind* (*Henry V Chorus*)

elbow, out at PHRASE out at elbow is an old phrase meaning in poor condition – as when your jacket sleeves are worn at the elbow which shows that it is an old jacket ❑ *He cannot, sir. He's out at elbow* (*Measure for Measure 2.1*)

element NOUN elements were thought to be the things from which all things were made. They were: air, earth, water and fire ❑ *Does not our lives consist of the four elements?* (*Twelfth Night 2.3*)

elf VERB to elf was to tangle ❑ *I'll ... elf all my hairs in knots* (*King Lear 2.3*)

embassy NOUN an embassy was a message ❑ *We'll once more hear Orsino's embassy.* (*Twelfth Night 1.5*)

emphasis NOUN emphasis here means a forceful expression or strong statement ❑ *What is he whose grief/ Bears such an emphasis* (*Hamlet 5.1*)

empiric NOUN an empiric was an untrained doctor sometimes called a quack ❑ *we must not ... prostitute our past-cure malady/ To empirics* (*All's Well That Ends Well 2.1*)

emulate ADJ emulate here means envious ❑ *pricked on by a most emulate pride* (*Hamlet 1.1*)

enchant VERB to enchant meant to put a magic spell on ❑ *Damn'd as thou art, thou hast enchanted her,/ For I'll refer me to all things of sense* (*Othello 1.2*)

enclog VERB to enclog was to hinder something or to provide an obstacle to it ❑ *Traitors enscarped to enclog the guitless keel* (*Othello 1.2*)

endure VERB to endure was to allow or to permit ❑ *and will endure/ Our setting down before't.* (*Macbeth 5.4*)

enfranchise VERB if you enfranchised something you set it free ❑ *Do this or this;/ Take in that kingdom and enfranchise that;/ Perform't, or else we damn thee.'* (*Anthony and Cleopatra 1.1*)

engage VERB to engage here means to pledge or to promise ❑ *This to be true I do engage my life* (*As You Like It 5.4*)

engaol VERB to lock up or put in prison ❑ *Within my mouth you have engaoled my tongue* (*Richard II 1.3*)

engine NOUN an engine was a plot, device or a machine ❑ *their promises, enticements, oaths, tokens, and all these engines, of lust, are not the things they go under* (*All's Well That Ends Well 3.5*)

englut VERB if you were engulfed you were swallowed up or eaten whole ❑ *For certainly thou art so near the gulf,/ Thou needs must be englutted.* (*Henry V 4.3*)

enjoined ADJ enjoined describes people joined together for the same reason ❑ *Of enjoined penitents/*

There's four or five (*All's Well That Ends Well* 3.5)

entertain 1 VERB to entertain here means to welcome or receive ❑ *Approach, rich Ceres, her to entertain.* (*The Tempest* 4.1) 2 VERB to entertain in this context means to cherish, hold in high regard or to respect ❑ *and I quake,/ Lest thou a feverous life shouldst entertain/ And six or seven winters more respect/ Than a perpetual honour.* (*Measure for Measure* 3.1) 3 VERB to entertain means here to give something consideration ❑ *But entertain it,/ And though you think me poor, I am the man/ Will give thee all the world.* (*Anthony and Cleopatra* 2.7) 4 VERB to entertain here means to treat or handle ❑ *your highness is not entertained with that ceremonious affection as you were wont* (*King Lear* 1.4)

envious ADJ envious meant spiteful or vindictive ❑ *he shall appear to the envious a scholar* (*Measure for Measure* 3.2)

ere PREP ere was a common word for before ❑ *ere this I should ha' fatted all the region kites* (*Hamlet* 2.2)

err VERB to err means to go astray, to make a mistake ❑ *And as he errs, doting on Hermia's eyes* (*A Midsummer Night's Dream* 1.1)

erst ADV erst was a common word for once or before ❑ *that erst brought sweetly forth/ The freckled cowslip* (*Henry V* 5.2)

eschew VERB if you eschew something you deliberately avoid doing it ❑ *What cannot be eschewed must be embraced* (*The Merry Wives of Windsor* 5.5)

escote VERB to escote meant to pay for, support ❑ *How are they escoted?* (*Hamlet* 2.2)

estimable ADJ estimable meant appreciative ❑ *I could not with such estimable wonder over-far believe that* (*Twelfth Night* 2.1)

extenuate VERB extenuate means to lessen ❑ *Which by no means we may extenuate* (*A Midsummer Night's Dream* 1.1)

fain ADV fain was a common word meaning gladly or willingly ❑ *I would fain prove so* (*Hamlet* 2.2)

fall NOUN in a voice or music fall meant going higher and lower ❑ *and so die/ That strain again! it had a dying fall* (*Twelfth Night* 1.1)

false ADJ false was a common word for treacherous ❑ *this is counter, you false Danish dogs!* (*Hamlet* 4.5)

fare VERB fare means to get on or manage ❑ *I fare well* (*The Taming of the Shrew Introduction* 2)

feign VERB to feign was to make up, pretend or fake ❑ *It is the more like to be feigned* (*Twelfth Night* 1.5)

fie EXCLAM fie was an exclamation of disgust ❑ *Fie, that you'll say so!* (*Twelfth Night* 1.3)

figure VERB to figure was to symbolize or look like ❑ *Wings and no eyes, figure unheedy haste* (*A Midsummer Night's Dream* 1.1)

filch VERB if you filch something you steal it ❑ *With cunning hast thou filch'd my daughter's heart* (*A Midsummer Night's Dream* 1.1)

flout VERB to flout something meant to scorn it ❑ *Why will you suffer her to flout me thus?* (*A Midsummer Night's Dream* 3.2)

fond ADJ fond was a common word meaning foolish ❑ *Shall we their fond pageant see?* (*A Midsummer Night's Dream 3.2*)

footing 1 NOUN footing meant landing on shore, arrival, disembarkation ❑ *Whose footing here anticipates our thoughts/A se'nnight's speed.* (*Othello 2.1*) 2 NOUN footing also means support ❑ *there your charity would have lacked footing* (*Winter's Tale 3.3*)

forsooth ADV in truth, certainly, truly ❑ *I had rather, forsooth, go before you like a man* (*The Merry Wives of Windsor 3.2*)

forswear VERB if you forswear you lie, swear falsely or break your word ❑ *he swore a thing to me on Monday night, which he forswore on Tuesday morning* (*Much Ado About Nothing 5.1*)

freshes NOUN a fresh is a fresh water stream ❑ *He shall drink nought brine, for I'll not show him/Where the quick freshes are.* (*Tempest 3.2*)

furlong NOUN a furlong is a measure of distance. It is the equivalent on one eight of a mile ❑ *Now would I give a thousand furlongs of sea for an acre of barren ground* (*Tempest 1.1*)

gaberdine NOUN a gaberdine is a cloak ❑ *My best way is to creep under his gaberdine* (*Tempest 2.2*)

gage NOUN a gage was a challenge to duel or fight ❑ *There is my gage, Aumerle, in gage to thine* (*Richard II 4.1*)

gait NOUN your gait is your way of walking or step ❑ *I know her by her gait* (*Tempest 4.1*)

gall VERB to gall is to annoy or irritate ❑ *Let it not gall your patience, good Iago,/That I extend my manners* (*Othello 2.1*)

gambol NOUN frolic or play ❑ *Hop in his walks, and gambol in his eyes* (*A Midsummer Night's Dream 3.1*)

gaskins NOUN gaskins is an old word for trousers ❑ *or, if both break, your gaskins fall.* (*Twelfth Night 1.5*)

gentle ADJ gentle means noble or well-born ❑ *thrice-gentle Cassio!* (*Othello 3.4*)

glass NOUN a glass was another word for a mirror ❑ *no woman's face remember/Save from my glass, mine own* (*Tempest 3.1*)

gleek VERB to gleek means to make a joke or jibe ❑ *Nay, I can gleek upon occasion* (*A Midsummer Night's Dream 3.1*)

gust NOUN gust meant taste, desire or enjoyment. We still say that if you do something with gusto you do it with enjoyment or enthusiasm ❑ *the gust he hath in quarrelling* (*Twelfth Night 1.3*)

habit NOUN habit means clothes ❑ *You know me by my habit* (*Henry V 3.6*)

heaviness NOUN heaviness means sadness or grief ❑ *So sorrow's heaviness doth heavier grow/For debt that bankrupt sleep doth sorrow owe* (*A Midsummer Night's Dream 3.2*)

heavy ADJ if you are heavy you are said to be sad or sorrowful ❑ *Away from light steals home my heavy son* (*Romeo and Juliet 1.1*)

hie VERB to hie meant to hurry ❑ *My husband hies him home* (*All Well That Ends Well 4.4*)

hollowly ADV if you did something hollowly you did it insincerely ❑ *If hollowly invert/ What best is boded me to mischief!* (*Tempest 3.1*)

holy-water, court PHRASE if you court holy water you make empty promises, or make statements which sound good but have no real meaning ❑ *court holy-water in a dry house is better than this rain-water out o'door* (*King Lear 3.2*)

howsoever ADV howsoever was often used instead of however ❑ *But howsoever strange and admirable* (*A Midsummer Night's Dream 5.1*)

humour NOUN your humour was your mood, frame of mind or temperament ❑ *it fits my humour well* (*As You Like It 3.2*)

ill ADJ ill means bad ❑ *I must thank him only,/ Let my remembrance suffer ill report* (*Antony and Cleopatra 2.2*)

indistinct ADJ inseparable or unable to see a difference ❑ *Even till we make the main and the aerial blue/ An indistinct regard.* (*Othello 2.1*)

indulgence NOUN indulgence meant approval ❑ *As you from crimes would pardoned be,/ Let your indulgence set me free* (*The Tempest Epilogue*)

infirmity NOUN infirmity was weakness or fraility ❑ *Be not disturbed with my infirmity* (*The Tempest 4.1*)

intelligence NOUN here intelligence means information ❑ *Pursue her; and for this intelligence/ If I have thanks* (*A Midsummer Night's Dream 1.1*)

inwards NOUN inwards meant someone's internal organs ❑ *the thought whereof/ Doth like a poisonous mineral gnaw my inwards* (*Othello 2.1*)

issue 1 NOUN the issue of a marriage are the children ❑ *To thine and Albany's issues,/ Be this perpetual* (*King Lear 1.1*) 2 NOUN in this context issue means outcome or result ❑ *I am to pray you, not to strain my speech,/ To grosser issues* (*Othello*)

kind NOUN kind here means situation or case ❑ *But in this kind, wanting your father's voice,/ The other must be held the worthier.* (*A Midsummer Night's Dream 1.1*)

knave NOUN a knave was a common word for scoundrel ❑ *How absolute the knave is!* (*Hamlet 5.1*)

league NOUN A distance. A league was the distance a person could walk in one hour ❑ *From Athens is her house remote seven leagues* (*A Midsummer Night's Dream 1.1*)

lief, had as ADJ I had as lief means I should like just as much ❑ *I had as lief the town crier spoke my lines* (*Hamlet 1.2*)

livery NOUN livery was a costume, outfit, uniform usually worn by a servant ❑ *You can endure the livery of a nun* (*A Midsummer Night's Dream 1.1*)

loam NOUN loam is soil containing decayed vegetable matter and therefore good for growing crops and plants ❑ *and let him have some plaster, or some loam, or some rough-cast about him, to signify wall* (*A Midsummer Night's Dream 3.1*)

lusty ADJ lusty meant strong ❑ *and oared/ Himself with his good arms in lusty stroke/ To th' shore* (*The Tempest 2.1*)

maidenhead NOUN maidenhead means chastity or virginity ❑ *What I am, and what I would, are as secret as maidenhead* (*Twelfth Night 1.5*)

mark VERB mark means to note or pay attention to ❑ *Where sighs and groans,/
Are made not marked* (*Macbeth 4.3*)

marvellous ADJ very or extremely ❑ *here's a marvellous convenient place for our rehearsal* (*A Midsummer Night's Dream 3.1*)

meet ADJ right or proper ❑ *tis most meet you should* (*Macbeth 5.1*)

merely ADV completely or entirely ❑ *Love is merely a madness* (*As You Like It 3.2*)

misgraffed ADJ misgraffed is an old word for mismatched or unequal ❑ *Or else misgraffed in respect of years* (*A Midsummer Night's Dream 1.1*)

misprision NOUN a misprision meant an error or mistake ❑ *Misprision in the highest degree!* (*Twelfth Night 1.5*)

mollification NOUN mollification is appeasement or a way of preventing someone getting angry ❑ *I am to hull here a little longer. Some mollification for your giant* (*Twelfth Night 1.5*)

mouth, cold in the PHRASE a well-known saying of the time which meant to be dead ❑ *What, must our mouths be cold?* (*The Tempest 1.1*)

murmur NOUN murmur was another word for rumour or hearsay ❑ *and then 'twas fresh in murmur* (*Twelfth Night 1.2*)

murrain NOUN murrain was another word for plague, pestilence ❑ *A murrain on your monster, and the devil take your fingers!* (*The Tempest 3.2*)

neaf NOUN neaf meant fist ❑ *Give me your neaf, Monsieur Mustardseed* (*A Midsummer Night's Dream 4.1*)

nice 1 ADJ nice had a number of meanings here it means fussy or particular ❑ *An therefore, goaded with most sharp occasions,/ Which lay nice manners by, I put you to/ The use of your own virtues* (*All's Well That Ends Well 5.1*) 2 ADJ nice here means critical or delicate ❑ *We're good... To set so rich a man/ On the nice hazard of one doubtful hour?* (*Henry IV part 1*) 3 ADJ nice in this context means carefully accurate, fastidious ❑ *O relation/ Too nice and yet too true!* (*Macbeth 4.3*) 4 ADJ trivial, unimportant ❑ *Romeo .. Bid him bethink/ How nice the quarrel was* (*Romeo and Juliet 3.1*)

nonpareil NOUN if you are nonpareil you are without equal, peerless ❑ *though you were crown'd/ The nonpareil of beauty!* (*Twelfth Night 1.5*)

office NOUN office here means business or work ❑ *Speak your office* (*Twelfth Night 1.5*)

outsport VERB outsport meant to overdo ❑ *Let's teach ourselves that honorable stop,/ Not to outsport discretion.* (*Othello 2.2*)

owe VERB owe meant own, possess ❑ *Lend less than thou owest* (*King Lear 1.4*)

paragon 1 VERB to paragon was to surpass or excede ❑ *he hath achieved a maid/ That paragons description and wild fame* (*Othello 2.1*) 2 VERB to paragon could also mean to compare with ❑ *I will give thee* *bloody teeth If thou with Caesar paragon again/ My man of men* (*Anthony and Cleopatra 1.5*)

pate NOUN pate is another word for head ❑ *Back, slave, or I will break thy pate across* (*The Comedy of Errors 2.1*)

paunch VERB to paunch someone is to stab (usually in the stomach). Paunch is still a common word for a stomach ❑ *Batter his skull, or paunch him with a stake* (*The Tempest 3.2*)

peevish ADJ if you are peevish you are irritable or easily angered ❑ *Run after that same peevish messenger* (*Twelfth Night 1.5*)

peradventure ADV perhaps or maybe ❑ *Peradventure this is not Fortune's work* (*As You Like It 1.2*)

perforce 1 ADV by force or violently ❑ *my rights and royalties,/ Plucked from my arms perforce* (*Richard II 2.3*) 2 ADV necessarily ❑ *The hearts of men, they must perforce have melted* (*Richard II 5.2*)

personage NOUN personage meant your appearance ❑ *Of what personage and years is he?* (*Twelfth Night 1.5*)

pestilence NOUN pestilience was a common word for plague or disease ❑ *Methought she purg'd the air of pestilence!* (*Twelfth Night 1.1*)

physic NOUN physic was medicine or a treatment ❑ *tis a physic/ That's bitter to sweet end* (*Measure for Measure 4.6*)

place NOUN place means a person's position or rank ❑ *Sons, kinsmen, thanes,/ And you whose places are the nearest* (*Macbeth 1.4*)

post NOUN here a post means a messenger ❑ *there are twenty weak and wearied posts/ Come from the north* (*Henry IV part II 2.4*)

pox NOUN pox was a word for any disease during which the victim had blisters on the skin. It was also a curse, a swear word ❑ *The pox of such antic, lisping, affecting phantasims* (*Romeo and Juliet 2.4*)

prate VERB to prate means to chatter ❑ *if thou prate of mountains* (*Hamlet 5.1*)

prattle VERB to prattle is to chatter or talk without purpose ❑ *I prattle out of fashion, and I dote In mine own comforts* (*Othello 2.1*)

precept NOUN a precept was an order or command ❑ *and my father's precepts I therein do forget.* (*The Tempest 3.1*)

present ADJ present here means immediate ❑ *We'll put the matter to the present push* (*Hamlet 5.1*)

prithee EXCLAM prithee is the equivalent of please or may I ask – a polite request ❑ *I prithee, and I'll pay thee bounteously* (*Twelfth Night 1.2*)

prodigal NOUN a prodigal is someone who wastes or squanders money ❑ *he's a very fool, and a prodigal* (*Twelfth Night 1.3*)

purpose NOUN purpose is used here to mean intention ❑ *understand my purposes aright* (*King Lear 1.4*)

quaff VERB quaff was a common word which meant to drink heavily or take a big drink ❑ *That quaffing and drinking will undo you* (*Twelfth Night 1.3*)

quaint 1 ADJ clever, ingenious ❑ *with a quaint device* (*The Tempest 3.3*) 2 ADJ cunning ❑ *I'll… tell quaint lies* (*Merchant of Venice 3.4*) 3 ADJ pretty, attractive ❑ *The clamorous owl, that nightly hoots and wonders/At our quaint spirit* (*A Midsummer Night's Dream 2.2*)

quoth VERB an old word which means say ❑ *Tis dinner time.' quoth I* (*The Comedy of Errors 2.1*)

rack NOUN a rack described clouds or a cloud formation ❑ *And, like this insubstantial pageant faded,/ Leave not a rack behind* (*The Tempest 4.1*)

rail VERB to rant or swear at. It is still used occasionally today ❑ *Why do I rail on thee* (*Richard II 5.5*)

rate NOUN rate meant estimate, opinion ❑ *My son is lost, and, in my rate, she too* (*The Tempest 2.1*)

recreant NOUN recreant is an old word which means coward ❑ *Come, recreant, come, thou child* (*A Midsummer Night's Dream 3.2*)

remembrance NOUN remembrance is used here to mean memory or recollection ❑ *our remembrances of days foregone* (*All's Well That Ends Well 1.3*)

resolute ADJ firm or not going to change your mind ❑ *You are resolute, then?* (*Twelfth Night 1.5*)

revels NOUN revels means celebrations or a party ❑ *Our revels now are ended* (*The Tempest 4.1*)

rough-cast NOUN a mixture of lime and gravel (sometimes shells too) for use on an outer wall ❑ *and let him have some plaster, or some loam, or some rough-cast about him, to signify wall* (*A Midsummer Night's Dream 3.1*)

sack NOUN sack was another word for wine ❑ *My man-monster hath drowned his tongue in sack.* (*The Tempest 3.2*)

sad ADJ in this context sad means serious, grave ❑ *comes me the Prince and Claudio… in sad conference* (*Much Ado About Nothing 1.3*)

sampler NOUN a piece of embroidery, which often showed the family tree ❑ *Both on one sampler, sitting on one cushion* (*A Midsummer Night's Dream 3.2*)

saucy ADJ saucy means rude ❑ *I heard you were saucy at my gates* (*Twelfth Night 1.5*)

schooling NOUN schooling means advice ❑ *I have some private schooling for you both.* (*A Midsummer Night's Dream 1.1*)

seething ADJ seething in this case means boiling – we now use seething when we are very angry ❑ *Lovers and madmen have such seething brains* (*A Midsummer Night's Dream 5.1*)

semblative ADJ semblative means resembling or looking like ❑ *And all is semblative a woman's part.* (*Twelfth Night 1.4*)

several ADJ several here means separate or different ❑ *twenty several messengers* (*Anthony and Cleopatra 1.5*)

shrew NOUN An annoying person or someone who makes you cross ❑ *Bless you, fair shrew.* (*Twelfth Night 1.3*)

shroud VERB to shroud is to hide or shelter ❑ *I will here, shroud till the dregs of the storm be past* (*The Tempest 2.2*)

sickleman NOUN a sickleman was someone who used a sickle to harvest crops ❑ *You sunburnt sicklemen, of August weary* (*The Tempest 4.1*)

soft ADV soft here means wait a moment or stop ❑ *But, soft, what nymphs are these* (*A Midsummer Night's Dream 4.1*)

something ADV something here means somewhat or rather ❑ *Be something scanter of your maiden presence* (*Hamlet 1.3*)

sooth NOUN truly ❑ *Yes, sooth; and so do you* (*A Midsummer Night's Dream 3.2*)

spleen NOUN spleen means fury or anger ❑ *That, in a spleen, unfolds both heaven and earth* (*A Midsummer Night's Dream 1.1*)

sport NOUN sport means recreation or entertainment ❑ *I see our wars/ Will turn unto a peaceful comic sport* (*Henry VI part I 2.2*)

strain NOUN a strain is a tune or a musical phrase ❑ *and so die/ That strain again! it had a dying fall* (*Twelfth Night 1.1*)

suffer VERB in this context suffer means perish or die ❑ *but an islander that hath lately suffered by a thunderbolt.* (*The Tempest 2.2*)

suit NOUN a suit is a petition, request or proposal (marriage) ❑ *Because she will admit no kind of suit* (*Twelfth Night 1.2*)

sup VERB to sup is to have supper ❑ *Go know of Cassio where he supped tonight* (*Othello 5.1*)

surfeit NOUN a surfeit is an amount which is too large ❑ *If music be the food of love, play on;/ Give me excess of it, that, surfeiting,/ The appetite may sicken* (*Twelfth Night 1.1*)

swain NOUN a swain is a suitor or person who wants to marry ❑ *take this transformed scalp/ From off the head of this Athenian swain* (*A Midsummer Night's Dream 4.1*)

thereto ADV thereto meant also ❑ *If she be black, and thereto have a wit* (*Othello 2.1*)

throstle NOUN a throstle was a name for a song-bird ❑ *The throstle with his note so true* (*A Midsummer Night's Dream 3.1*)

tidings NOUN tidings meant news ❑ *that upon certain tidings now arrived, importing the mere perdition of the Turkish fleet* (*Othello 2.2*)

transgress VERB if you transgress you break a moral law or rule of behaviour ❑ *Virtue that transgresses is but patched with sin* (*Twelfth Night 1.5*)

troth, by my PHRASE this phrase means I swear or in truth or on my word ❑ *By my troth, Sir Toby, you must come in earlier o' nights* (*Twelfth Night 1.3*)

trumpery NOUN trumpery means things that look expensive but are worth nothing (often clothing) ❑ *The trumpery in my house, go bring it hither/ For stale catch these thieves* (*The Tempest 4.1*)

twink NOUN In the wink of an eye or no time at all ❑ *Ay, with a twink* (*The Tempest 4.1*)

undone ADJ if something or someone is undone they are ruined, destroyed, brought down ❑ *You have undone a man of fourscore three* (*The Winter's Tale 4.4*)

varlets NOUN varlets were villains or ruffians ❑ *Say again: where didst thou leave these varlets?* (*The Tempest 4.1*)

vaward NOUN the vaward is an old word for the vanguard, front part or earliest ❑ *And since we have the vaward of the day* (*A Midsummer Night's Dream 4.1*)

visage NOUN face ❑ *when Phoebe doth behold/ Her silver visage in the watery glass* (*A Midsummer Night's Dream 1.1*)

voice NOUN voice means vote ❑ *He has our voices* (*Coriolanus 2.3*)

waggish ADJ waggish means playful ❑ *As waggish boys in game themselves forswear* (*A Midsummer Night's Dream 1.1*)

wane VERB to wane is to vanish, go down or get slighter. It is most often used to describe a phase of the moon ❑ *but, O, methinks, how slow/ This old moon wanes* (*A Midsummer Night's Dream 1.1*)

want VERB to want means to lack or to be without ❑ *a beast that wants discourse of reason/ Would have mourned longer* (*Hamlet 1.2*)

warrant VERB to assure, promise, guarantee ❑ *I warrant your grace* (*As You Like It 1.2*)

welkin NOUN welkin is an old word for the sky or the heavens ❑ *The starry welkin cover thou anon/ With drooping fog as black as Acheron* (*A Midsummer Night's Dream 3.2*)

wench NOUN wench is an old word for a girl ❑ *Well demanded, wench* (*The Tempest 1.2*)

whence ADV from where ❑ *Whence came you, sir?* (*Twelfth Night 1.5*)

wherefore ADV why ❑ *Wherefore, sweetheart? what's your metaphor?* (*Twelfth Night 1.3*)

wide-chopped ADJ if you were wide-chopped you were big-mouthed ❑ *This wide-chopped rascal* (*The Tempest 1.1*)

wight NOUN wight is an old word for person or human being ❑ *She was a wight, if ever such wight were* (*Othello 2.1*)

wit NOUN wit means intelligence or wisdom ❑ *thou didst conclude hairy men plain dealers, without wit* (*The Comedy of Errors 2.2*)

wits NOUN wits mean mental sharpness ❑ *we that have good wits have much to answer for* (*As You Like It 4.1*)

wont ADJ to wont is to be in the habit of doing something regularly ❑ *When were you wont to use my sister thus?* (*The Comedy of Errors 2.2*)

wooer NOUN a wooer is a suitor, someone who is hoping to marry ❑ *and of a foolish knight that you brought in one night here to be her wooer* (*Twelfth Night 1.3*)

wot VERB wot is an old word which means know or learn ❑ *for well I wot/ Thou runnest before me* (*A Midsummer Night's Dream 3.2*)